Of Valentines and Vendetta

A BRIGHTON VILLAGE COZY MYSTERY

SYLVIE KURTZ

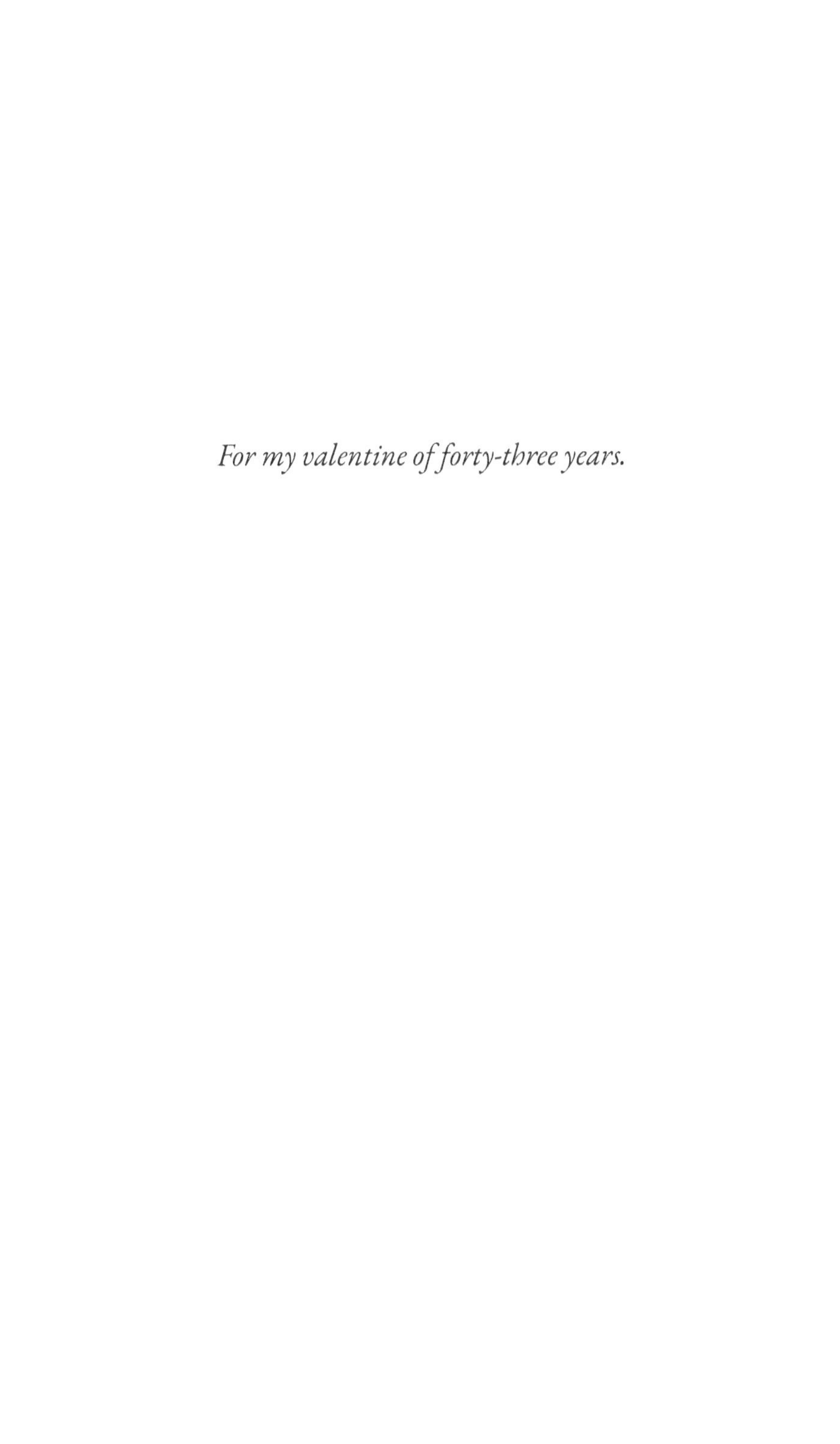

For my valentine of forty-three years.

ONE

A Bitter Anniversary

Valentine's Day. The most awful day of the year. Men felt pressure to put on grand romantic gestures. Women, to act out their lovers' fantasies. And then, when they inevitably disappointed each other, tempers flared, punches flew, people died.

Snow gusted outside the kitchen window, wind splaying hunks of white against the panes. The wind wailed around the trees in the yard, shaking the branches, reflecting the never-ending howl living in my chest. At the counter in the too-warm kitchen, I added the wet ingredients to the dry in the bowl and beat them with too much vigor.

Harlan, my Harlan, was lying dead in a grave. The murderer's wife had suffered surgery after surgery to rebuild her shattered face. And the drunken monster who maimed his lover and killed my husband had gotten to live. Why was life so unfair?

Seventy-three police officers had died responding to domestic disturbance calls last year. The highest number recorded by the FBI, which kept track of such things. The number grew every year. That didn't count the officers who were assaulted and survived. That number had ballooned over the hundred thousand mark. Their arrival at an already unstable scene lit the fuse that quickly flamed out of control.

Not even the scent of cinnamon could stop the tears from flowing down my face and into the muffin batter. Again.

A year since Harlan had died, and it still felt as if the knock on the door had happened yesterday. Instead of the delivery of a bouquet of pink Gerbera daisies with yellow hearts (my favorites—I know, kinda common, but I loved the cheerfulness of them), a cordon of cops had stood at my door. And I knew, of course I knew, because so many officers looking so somber could mean only one thing: someone had died. And if they were on my doorstep and Harlan wasn't? Well, it didn't take a genius to figure out the math.

Stella Luna hopped up from her faux-shearling-lined bed in the corner by the sliding glass door just as the front door blew open and my sister-in-law Page blustered in, bringing in half the storm with her. Tail beating like an old-fashioned washing machine, Stella raced up the hallway to greet Page with happy yips and licks.

"You won't believe what happened," Page shouted at me from the front door, stomping the snow off her boots on the dirt-and-water-catching door mat.

"What are you doing out in a storm?" I scooped up a spoonful of too-dense banana bread batter, then let it drop back into the bowl. These muffins would turn out like concrete. And yet, I kept going as if they would bake up light and fluffy. "You should be home."

Having shed her coat, hat and scarf along the way, Page appeared in the kitchen, her tawny hair more of a rat's nest than a bun. She wore a crazy red-pink-and-purple heart sweater that had my throat clogging and tears ready to flow again.

"I run a business, you know." Page petted Stella, who insisted on licking her hands.

I turned away from her and added chocolate chips to the banana muffin batter—as if that would help the disaster it was. "Nobody's venturing out to your bookstore today."

In my peripheral vision, I caught her shaking her head at the table covered with baked goods and tutting. "This can't go on, Ellie."

I shrugged. Today's output was enormous, even by my

standards. A year today. Did Page not remember? "It's how I cope."

"I'm saying this as someone who cares for you like a sister." She came up behind me and folded me in a hug and a cloud of her apple-and-orange shampoo. "You should see someone."

"It didn't help." I shrugged her off. The three things I'd learned from my brief stab at grief counseling were that grief was individual, that you couldn't rush the process, that the sadness would lessen in its own time.

"There are grief groups," Page said.

"Do you know how depressing those places are? People crying, talking about the people they miss in some dark church basement."

"Healing themselves as they talk." With a sigh, she reached into a cupboard and plucked out a mug. Stella waited patiently by Page's chair for her return.

"I've never been a group person. Besides, I don't like driving at night anymore, especially in winter."

Page filled her mug with coffee from the machine and added half the sugar bowl to the brew. "Well, I came here for some sympathy. Looks like I found my solution instead."

"A solution to what?"

"My baker didn't show up this morning."

"Nobody's going to show up today, Page."

"Townies will." She went to a bottom cupboard and retrieved several 9 x 13-inch plastic containers. "They always pack the place on stormy days."

"Help yourself." I yanked a muffin tin from the drying rack, then lined the cups with paper liners.

"I will." She filled three containers with bars and cookies and two muffin caddies with muffins and cupcakes, then plopped down onto a kitchen chair and sipped her coffee, absently petting Stella's too-long hair. The mutt was overdue for a haircut. Yet another untouched to-do item on my long list.

"Like my granny used to say," Page said, "the more you do a villain a favor, the more he craps in your hands."

"I doubt your granny ever said that."

"Worse, actually, but I know how you feel about swearing. She had a foul mouth, Granny H did."

I'd never met the woman, but Harlan had mentioned she'd been a character. I guessed Page came by her quirkiness through DNA. I scooped the thick muffin batter into the liners. "Who did you do a favor for?"

"Gayle Chapman Chilton. She asked me to hire her daughter fresh out of baking school." Page shook her head and tutted. "Last time I listen to the mother about how talented her offspring is, even if she has the pull to slow my business to a crawl. I had a terrific baker lined up, too, and had to turn her away. I'm no good at politics." Page peeled the wrapper from an apple walnut muffin. "And now, after less than six months, I may have to sack the girl. She just isn't reliable enough."

This, from the woman who was the ultimate representation of unreliable. Then I had to take back my assessment. When it came to the bookstore, you could count on Page. And when it came to having a shoulder to cry on, she was there too. I shoved the muffin tin into the oven and set a timer.

Mouth still full of muffin, Page said, "These are so good." She glanced around at the table, eyebrows popping up. "You should come be my baker." She shoved the half-eaten muffin in my direction, then back at her chest. "Win-win."

A spiral of something wild whirled in my chest. "No, Page. I can't."

"Why not? What else are you going to do with all these baked goods? If you're going to bake anyway... I'd pay for your supplies."

"I don't want you thinking I can show up every day." Because some days were harder than others. Some days, I couldn't get out of bed. Some days, the tears never stopped.

"Oh, Ellie."

"Today is—" I started, then couldn't squeak out

anything more. The hole in my heart was so big I thought it might swallow me whole.

"I know," Page said, voice somber. She stood, then wrapped her arms around me. We clung to each other as if our connecting skeletons were the only way to stay upright. Stella whined at our feet. "One year. Why do you think I need to keep busy too?"

Hence, the venturing out in a storm. "We're a pair, aren't we?"

I didn't know how long we stayed like that, tears soaking each other's shoulders. Finally, Page pulled away, wiping her wet cheeks with the sleeve of her sweater. "I'm going to take these." She pointed at the muffins, cookies and cupcakes mounded on the table. "Freeze what I can't use today."

I nodded. The oven beeper went off. I opened the oven door. A wave of heat hit my face.

I couldn't stay here.

Not today.

Not with part of me expecting a knock on the door. And I didn't want to see Nolan Lander. Not at all. I didn't want to see his grief-grooved face. I didn't want to hear his words of comfort. I didn't want to feel his sadness. I had enough of my own.

And Harlan's best friend would come check on me today because he and Harlan had made a pact a long time ago to take care of each other's families should one of them die in the line of duty.

"I'll go with you," I said to Page, working through the knot in my throat. "In case the bookstore is busy." I turned off the oven and shot her a poor attempt at a smile over my shoulder. "Or you run your car into a snowbank."

LUNCHTIME BROUGHT A FRESH WAVE OF customers. I'd been running from the moment Page opened The Purple Page Bookshop at nine, serving baked goods, coffee, tea and hot chocolate as if we were the only place in town to get food, which we weren't. Every table was filled. People sat cross-legged on the floor of the bookstore, sipping drinks, eating muffins and reading books. That, in my opinion, was a dangerous combination. But Page seemed to think it brought sales.

Stella wandered through the crowd on the bookstore side, seeking pats and treats, then snoozed under the checkout counter.

On the plus side, I was too busy to think. On the minus side, my feet throbbed, and my shoulders ached. I tried to insert the portafilter into the brew head on the cappuccino machine, but it wouldn't go in. Why had Page had to get such a complicated contraption to brew a simple cup of coffee? She didn't own a coffee shop; she was a bookstore owner, for heaven's sake. I jabbed at it again.

"Do you want some help with that?"

A young woman stood at the counter, swaddled in a puffy olive-green parka, resting bothered face in place, impatience sparking in her eyes.

"I've got it, thanks." *Jab, jab, jab.* Why wasn't it fitting? Why did everyone want a complicated coffee?

She came around the counter, took the portafilter from me and inserted it into the brew head as if the thing were greased. She then placed a cup under the tap, then pressed a button, and the machine purred into action. She gave me a small smile. "There."

"Thanks."

"I'm Bailey Hale."

"Uh, thanks, Bailey."

Her brows lifted. "From the temp agency? Page Hamlin wanted someone for the day because of the Chocolate Festival?" She cocked her head. "Here I am."

I'd forgotten about the Chocolate Festival—the two-day chocolate trail that went from store to store and left the town on a caffeine high for a week. "I thought it was postponed until next weekend due to the snow."

"But the order for extra help at the agency wasn't canceled, so here I am." She gazed around the crowded store decorated with hearts and cupids and roses. Lace doilies decorated every open surface. Chocolate hearts overflowed from fancy bowls all over the store. "Looks like you could use some help."

I pointed my chin toward the crowded checkout counter on the bookstore side. "Page is over there."

Bailey gave a sharp nod and headed for Page. Help would be nice, especially if she ran the stupid coffee machine.

A few minutes later, while I was struggling with another fancy coffee order, Page whistled, getting my attention. The heart antennas on her Valentine's headband wobbled like manic ladybugs. She pointed at Bailey and gave me a thumbs-up, then sent Bailey my way.

"Where do you want me?" Bailey unzipped her parka.

"The machine seems to like you. You're in charge of coffee orders." I nodded toward the hooks on the back of the door that separated the café from the bookstore. "You can hang your coat and bag over there."

She did so without a word, then slid right into the job as if it had been hers forever. I liked that she didn't feel the need to fill every moment with annoying chitchat or questions.

Bailey and I worked seamlessly for the rest of the day. She served drinks. I took care of baked goods. Then, along with Page, we all collapsed into chairs after closing.

"That was a day." Page swept her frizzy hair up and attempted to stuff it back into a bun.

"It was," I agreed. I needed a hot shower and sleep, but the thought of going home to my empty house filled me with dread. "I'll take care of the cleanup."

"You will not," Page said, yawning. "I'll help."

Good, I didn't want to be alone.

"I can help too." Bailey sat up straight in her chair fresh and perky as if she were just starting the day rather than ending it. Not a hair was out of place on the dark-brown bun beneath her hairnet.

Page waved her offer away. "You've done so much already, Bailey."

"It's no problem."

Page popped forward in her chair, and I could almost see the lightbulb turning on above her head. "Do you want a job?"

I kicked Page under the table and goggled at her. Was she forgetting that Kady was still her baker/manager?

Page frowned. "What?"

"Don't you have something to do first?"

She rolled her eyes. "If a job were to become available to run the café, would you be interested?"

Bailey smiled her first genuine smile. "I would."

"Can you bake?"

"I have a degree in baking and pastry arts from the Institute of Culinary Education in New York."

"Impressive," Page said.

"Why would you want to work in a small café in a nowhere town?" Yes, part of me was always on guard for someone trying to take advantage of Page. She was too kind for her own good and often ended up giving more than she got back.

"My family's here."

Page nodded. Her family was down to me and my kids. We meant everything to her.

"Where?"

"The wrong side of the tracks." The look in her eye dared me to make something of it. "I grew up in the trailer park."

Another hit in Page's too-soft armor. Page patted her hand. "Drop off a résumé on Monday."

Bailey's lips curved into a small smile. "Thanks."

I got up, and my knees creaked. "Let's get to it."

I scrubbed the kitchen while Page and Bailey filled garbage bags, lined them up at the back door, then swept and swabbed the floor in the café. The chairs were turned up on the tables, the cappuccino machine was cleaned, and the scent of lemon dishwashing soap lingered in the air.

"All right," I said, hand on the small of my aching back. "Let's get these out, then we can go home."

Page and I each grabbed a bag. Bailey grabbed two.

"Can I go home with you?" Page used her padded hips to push open the back door. "I don't want to be alone tonight."

The wintery bluster rushed in like an assault, cooling the warmth of the kitchen. Outside, only the single security bulb above the back door lit the alley, casting it in stark shadows.

"Where's Bert?" Bert Brewster was Page's long-time boyfriend. Every year on Valentine's Day, he asked her to marry him. Every year, she said no. They lived in separate houses, which I found odd, but Page said it worked for them. Who was I to judge when they seemed happy with the arrangement?

"Stuck at the airport in Chicago due to weather."

Bert traveled a lot for his job as a business consultant. "Sorry."

"It's for the best." Page sighed. "I couldn't stand a proposal today."

I got that. I couldn't stand the sight of flowers or cops today. I just wanted to fall into a deep sleep and wake up from this living nightmare to find Harlan on his side of the bed, snoring softly.

Page stopped and tapped the heel of her hand on her temple. "I forgot the compost."

She launched her bag into the dumpster. "I'll be right back."

I followed with mine. Bailey tried to toss both at once. One fell back, nearly bowling Page over as she reached for the shop's door. The other got hung up on the lip, stuck just out of reach.

"I'll go get the step stool." I grabbed the white two-step stool Page kept in the kitchen, then went back outside.

I was about to climb the thing when Bailey took it from me. "I got the bag stuck. I'll do it."

Bailey shoved at the side of the bag, trying to tip it in. The bag ripped, spilling refuse all over the alley. "Sorry!"

"I'll get another bag." Page placed the compost bin with the coffee grinds on the snow beside the door and went back inside.

Bailey grabbed as much of the hanging spillage as she could. Standing at the top of the step stool, an armful of refuse staining her white apron brown, she froze.

Then she screamed.

TWO

The Easy Answer

ailey tripped on her way down the stepstool in the narrow alley behind the bookshop. Refuse spilled from her shaking arms, and she couldn't stop screaming.

I climbed up on the stepstool to see what had made her scream. And there, couched by the harsh shadows of the security light: a face. White flour and discarded red heart confetti decorated the skin like a piece of speculative art. A black garbage bag covered the body like a blanket. The eyes were wide open but unseeing. Something spilled out of the mouth. I leaned closer. Chocolate-covered coffee beans. I'd seen a half-filled jar of them in the café's kitchen. My heart beat in double time, and my palms grew sweaty in spite of the cold. My mind couldn't hang on to any thought, except that this wouldn't be good.

Page folded the shaking and sobbing Bailey into her arms and looked up at me, fear rounding her eyes. "What's wrong?"

"I think we found your baker."

"Kady?"

I nodded, then pulled my phone out of my jeans pocket. It took my fingers a couple of tries to dial 9-1-1.

While Page took Bailey inside, I zipped up my fleece jacket and stood by the dumpster, waiting for Nolan Lander, the acting chief of police. He'd stepped into Harlan's job less than a week after his murder. This, in spite of his assertion that he didn't want the job. He said he'd done it for me, for the kids. But he'd always competed with Harlan in subtle ways. Had he done anything to find a replacement? No.

Nolan arrived five minutes later, unfolding his tall body from the cruiser as if it were a clown car. He strode toward me with the permanent hunch of a man used to folding himself through doorways to avoid hitting his head. I hated that he was here and Harlan wasn't.

"What happened?" he asked, facing me, his narrowed gaze studying my face with his eerie golden eyes. I hated that he looked at me with such pity. I hated that I could feel his grief.

And that hatred boiled into anger I took out on him. "Isn't that what *you're* supposed to figure out?"

His jaw flinched as if he chewed back a tart retort. "You mentioned a body."

Yep, he was the bigger man. Which was no doubt why I used him as my emotional punching bag.

"Page's baker didn't show up for work. It was a busy day, so I came to help out Page. We were cleaning up. A garbage bag got hung up." I pointed at the sharp lip of the dumpster. "When Bailey went up to push it in, she screamed and tumbled down. I went to see why and saw the missing baker lying there, dead."

"Bailey?"

"Bailey Hale, a temp for the day because of the Chocolate Festival even though it was postponed."

He made a note and nodded. "The baker?"

"Kady Chilton."

His gaze snapped up. "As in Gayle Chapman Chilton's daughter?"

"As in." Dr. Gayle Chapman Chilton headed the cardiology department at the Hopewell Community Hospital. She wielded a lot of influence in the area and would use all of it against the police department, Page, and anyone who got in the way of putting her daughter's murderer in prison. Suddenly cold, I rubbed my arms against the chill of the night.

Nolan placed a wide hand against the small of my back

and pushed me toward the door. "Why don't you go sit inside with Page while I take a look around?"

I balked and held my ground. "I'd like to stay."

"Ellie..."

"I—" I closed my eyes and shook my head. Valentine's Day. Harlan. Another murder. "I need to."

After another one of his long scrutinizing looks, he let out a resigned breath. "Stay out of the way."

"I always do."

He snorted and turned his back on me, setting his laser gaze on the inside of the dumpster.

———

NOLAN CHATTED WITH PAGE AND BAILEY WHILE the crime scene team, looking like yetis in the snow, did their thing out in the alley. He had an officer drive Bailey home, but Page insisted on driving herself, along with Stella, to my house. Then he sat on a high stool by the big stainless steel table, scrubbed and mirror-shiny.

Even though we'd already cleaned the coffee contraption, I bounced up from my own stool and made coffee to keep my hands busy.

"How are you holding up?" Nolan's gaze pierced right through my back.

No, no, no, we were *not* going there. Instead of

answering him, I ground some beans, letting the whirring sound drown his words. I didn't want to talk about my feelings. Or his. I didn't want to talk about Harlan. Certainly not with Nolan. Or here at the scene of yet another crime.

I watched the coffee drip into the mug as if it needed all of my attention, then handed the mug to Nolan. Black. No sugar. No cream. Just like Harlan. He'd told me once that if you took your coffee black, you were never disappointed. I still liked a little cream in mine. As frayed as my nerves were right now, the last thing I needed was coffee, but I went ahead and made myself a cup anyway.

"You can't avoid me forever," Nolan said. The big mug looked like a child's in his hands.

"I can try."

He sighed. "I'd have traded places with him in a minute. You know that."

That only made it worse. I needed to hate him. It was the only thing that made this situation bearable.

He took a slug of coffee. "Way better than the cop shop's coffee."

"It's all in the beans."

He jutted his chin toward the alley. "What do you know about Kady?"

A small huff of relief escaped me. He was changing subjects. For now. "Not much. She came through the school system after Cammy and Evie but before R.J." My son had insisted that he couldn't live up to either of his names—Remy (my dead brother) and Jamison (the lawyer who'd saved my brother and me as teens)—and on his twentieth birthday had insisted he wanted to be called R.J. from then on. "Part of the 'it' girl crowd. On the quiet side, not the leader of the pack."

I hadn't worked at the middle school since R.J. had graduated, so I wasn't up on all the school gossip.

"Know anyone who'd want her dead?" Nolan asked, those golden eyes piercing like a bobcat's with prey in sight.

My eyebrows rose. "Why would I? I haven't seen the girl in years."

"What about Page?"

"What about her?"

He ground his back teeth together. "Does she have a motive to kill her baker?"

"Page? Really? The woman who marches ants and spiders out the door rather than squish them?"

His gaze went up to the shelf where the half-full jar of chocolate-covered coffee beans rested front and center. Like the ones that filled Kady's mouth. Why had someone done that? Why had they strewn flour and heart confetti all over her dead body?

"You know, you've got to stop trying to fit round pegs

into square holes. Page gave a newbie baker the chance to run the café because she was a local girl."

"With an influential mother—"

"And the girl was constantly late. But Page is nothing if not kind and forgiving and kept giving her chances. Page was thinking that she'd have to fire her, but she wouldn't kill her over tardiness."

He nodded as if I'd said something profound. I wanted to punch him. "We both know she's impulsive."

"Okay, then, let me do your job for you." I leaned forward. "Check to see if she had a boyfriend. It's always the partner, isn't it?"

He had the good grace to flinch, given how Harlan had died. "Did she? Have a boyfriend?"

"How should I know? I've barely left my house in a year."

"And yet, here you are, out, on this day of all days."

"Because the house was closing in on me and I didn't want to have to deal with you."

"Yet, here we are."

"Like the flu, I can't avoid you."

"Elize."

I shook my head. "Don't 'Elize' me." I pointed a finger at him. "Let me give you more leads to follow since you seem hell-bent on closing the case before you even investigate. Check the mother's alibi. Gayle Chapman Chilton seemed to take great pleasure in putting her daughter down."

"I thought you weren't up on gossip."

I rolled my eyes. "Gossip finds me anyway."

"She put pressure on Page to hire her daughter."

So Page had told him that. The woman had no filter, and that would get her in trouble. "Check to see if any of the mean girls are still in town and if they've had a falling out with the privileged princess. Check Hopewell College. She was part of the first baking and pastry arts graduating class. See how she got along there. Check—"

"I get the gist."

I leaned forward and narrowed my gaze at him, my whole body buzzing. I had to stop drinking so much coffee. "Maybe *I* had a motive to kill her."

He didn't even flinch. "Did you?"

"Of course not!" I had to clamp my hands around the mug to keep myself from throwing the contents at him.

"You're very protective of Page."

"Someone has to look out for her now that Harlan's gone." Anger turned into a revving engine in my gut. "Harlan would roll over in his grave knowing you even thought Page could do something like that."

"Harlan would look at every possibility, even if it included his own wife and sister."

That hit me like a slap and my whole body jolted.

Because Nolan was right. A few Halloweens ago, Harlan'd had his own daughter brought in for questioning.

The job, the blasted job, always came first.

I grabbed my coat and purse and headed for the front door.

"Where are you going?" He released the mug as if he'd use the hand to reel me back in.

"Home."

"You don't have a car."

"I'll walk." I crossed the café's floor and pulled on the front door, letting in a blast of icy air. Anything was better than being locked up in the too-tight space of a car with this man. One of us wouldn't arrive alive. "Lock up when you're done here."

"Ellie."

I put a hand up to stop his forward motion toward me. "Don't. I don't want to be anywhere near you right now."

"Okay." He put up his hands in defeat, then pulled out his phone and had the officer on duty at the PD come collect me and take me home.

Before making my exit, during which I planned to slam the door with everything I had, I warned him, "I will *not* let you take the easy way out and blame Page for something she didn't do."

THREE

The Wrong Suspect

That late cup of coffee had me too wired to sleep. I checked in with each of the kids to see how they were doing on the anniversary of their father's death. Cammy didn't want to talk; she never did. Evie talked my ear off for almost an hour. And R. J. grunted at me, insisting he was fine. They'd all taken their father's murder hard and each was struggling in their own way. Cammy buried herself in work. Evie, still fresh from her fiancé's murder a few Halloweens ago, couldn't seem to focus on anything except her kindergarten kids. R.J.'s grades had slipped. They didn't want me to worry about them, but how could I not?

Page sat on the couch in my living room with Stella Luna half in her lap and a rainbow-colored, granny square blanket wrapped over her head and around her shoulders, looking like a creature from a horror movie. No, more like defeated. And that wasn't like Page. With everything she'd gone through in her life—from her parents' tragic deaths at an early age to being left at the altar—she'd somehow managed to keep an optimistic outlook on life. A foil to my own glass-half-empty view.

Now that Harlan was gone, it was up to me to look after Page. I wouldn't let him down.

"I can't believe Kady's dead." Page petted one of Stella's floppy ears. Stella nuzzled closer, sighing in contentment. She was supposed to be my dog, but somehow she ended up being Harlan's and now seemed to prefer Page. "I feel bad for being mad at her for being late."

"You couldn't have known." Kady's body had gone to the morgue for an autopsy a few hours ago, but the shock of her death still weighed like wet snow after a storm. Every time I closed my eyes, I saw the young woman lying in the dumpster behind the shop, her black garbage bag blanket, her flour-white skin with shiny red hearts dotting her cheeks and those chocolate-covered espresso beans spilling out of her mouth.

This wasn't random. This was personal. Someone had posed her that way. Someone wanted her to pay for some sort of perceived crime. Someone was sending a message.

I'd watched the crime scene team pick through the dumpster and bag evidence, including a rolling pin from the café's kitchen. Never mind that Page didn't know how to bake and had left that side of the business completely to Kady. They'd bagged ripped paper, reading glasses I recognized as Page's—glasses she was forever losing, which was why she owned half a dozen pairs—an apron with what looked like dried blood on the bib and a set of keys. Again, Page didn't bake; she didn't wear an apron. All these items felt like plants—as if someone wanted Page to pay for Kady's death. But why?

I sucked in a breath. Maybe Kady wasn't the point. Maybe someone had some sort of vendetta against Page. Which didn't make sense. But neither did the evidence.

The crime scene team had photographed every angle of the alley and dumpster, including the security camera that they'd most likely learned wasn't working and hadn't since the ice storm over the holidays. Repairing it wasn't a priority. After all, this was Brighton Village not the big city.

I hadn't known Kady well, practically not at all. But she was gone. And Page, by all appearances, was Nolan's prime—and only—suspect. As if he hadn't known her since she was a kid. As if he weren't practically a second brother.

I plugged in the kettle, then got out two teal ceramic mugs and two bags of chamomile tea. "We need to figure out how long she was in that dumpster."

Because Nolan wasn't going to look farther than the

end of his nose to close the case. If Page were to go free, I'd have to find the killer and bring him or her to justice tied in a neat bow. The kettle shrieked and I filled the mugs with hot water. "When was the last time you saw her?"

Page accepted the mug I handed her, hunching over the steam as if that could warm her cold core. "At closing. Last night. No two nights ago. She asked for Friday off because I was asking her to work longer hours over the weekend because of the Chocolate Festival."

"So, Thursday night?"

Page nodded. "I had her bake extra for Friday since she wasn't going to be there. I had Janelle work the café counter."

Janelle was Page's recently hired part-time clerk. If I was a glass-half-empty person, then Janelle was an empty-glass person. I didn't think I'd ever seen her smile, and she put out an aura of negative energy. Not that I believed in woo-woo the way Page did, but Janelle's negativity smothered like a wave of humid air. I told Page that wasn't good for business, but Page with her soft heart, had told me to leave it alone.

"Kady wanted to tinker with a new recipe for the Chocolate Festival." Page's lips trembled. "She said she liked the quiet there in the café's kitchen."

"Did she do that often? Stay after hours?"

Page toggled her head from side to side. "Often

enough. I think she liked being alone here." Page snorted. "Away from her mother."

Dr. Chapman Chilton wanted things her way, and her only child had fallen short of expectations. "She lived at home?"

"The carriage house behind Chapel Hill."

"And you've put garbage in that dumpster since then?" I sat next to her and Stella batted my thighs with her flag tail.

"Of course. I recycle the cardboard and paper, and compost as much of the food as I can, but there's still a lot of garbage every day between the café and the bookstore."

"So, she hadn't been there for those two days. If she had, she'd have been covered with garbage, not lying right at the top where we found her." Had she been killed elsewhere and moved to the dumpster? Had someone wanted her to be found? I blew on the tea, then watched the surface ripple. "Walk me through your day at the shop before you drove to my house in the middle of a storm."

Page curled even more around the mug, drawing the blanket tighter around her shoulders with one hand, hunching like a fairytale crone. "I got into the shop at around seven thirty as usual. Did the regular things—turned on the lights, the computers, checked the messages. Kady's supposed to get there around six to start baking for the nine a.m. opening."

"She wasn't there."

"Nope. The café was dark."

"Did you call her right away?"

The blanket head moved from side to side. "With the storm, I gave her extra time to get there because she lives out in the country. She didn't answer. After I got everything ready for the bookshop's opening, I called her again. Still no answer."

She lifted the mug, but as if it were too heavy, she let it sink back to her lap. "By then, I was in a mood. Not just because Kady was late again, but...you know."

"Harlan." Just saying his name was like pouring vinegar on an open wound.

She nodded and winced as she attempted a sip of the too-hot tea. "I gave her three chances to answer. She didn't. That's when I decided I needed to fire her and hire someone else. Then I went to see if you wanted to bake until I hired a new baker. With the storm, I knew it was going to be a busy day. And if I had baked goods, people would stay longer." She lifted both shoulders. "You were there for the rest."

"So, you were alone in the store for about an hour before you left again." Most likely driving her "batmobile" too fast, making it look as if she were fleeing the scene of the crime should anyone have happened to see her. That wouldn't look good for her innocence because it gave her means and opportunity. And Nolan would see a motive where there wasn't one.

Page sighed. "Sounds about right."

"Was her coat, her purse, anything there to show she'd come in for another stealth baking session?"

Page frowned. "I didn't notice anything, but then I wasn't looking." She tapped her lips with a finger. "She likes to keep her stuff in one of the bins because she doesn't like flour all over her street clothes."

"We need to get back in the shop." We needed to see whether her stuff was still there.

Page turtled down even more. "Think the police are done?"

Unfortunately for Page, I was pretty sure they were putting a bow on her guilt and getting ready to bring her in for questioning. "By morning, for sure."

The chamomile wasn't doing anything to bring me closer to sleep. I put the mug down on the coffee table, disturbing Stella, who gave me the side-eye. "We need to find out what Nolan knows."

"How?"

"I don't know. Yet."

———

Sleep wouldn't come. I stared at the ceiling for of what was left of the night. Even Stella couldn't stand the racket of my thoughts and left, most likely to find Page, who was camping out in the girls' room.

I got up, then stopped at Harlan's office door. I hadn't opened it in a year. That way, I could pretend he was in there, working on a case. My throat bobbed. In his office, maybe I could feel him there, ask him for help to free his sister. Breath held, I turned the knob. Stale and still air assaulted my nose. Beneath that, the undertone of his piney soap. My heart grew heavy in my chest, and I put a hand to it, as if that could stop the pain.

Light from the hallway spilled in, outlining the filing cabinets along the back wall, the metal desk in front of those cabinets, the whiteboard across from the desk. Having known I'd leave him his favorite peanut butter cookies on his desk—the plastic-wrapped plate was still there—he'd drawn a big heart with an arrow across it with H. H. H. on one side and E. D. H. on the other. My whole body sagged, and I closed the door before I crumpled on the floor and started crying.

I went to the kitchen, poured two mugs of coffee and took a seat at the kitchen table where I'd sat so often with Harlan, talking—well, mostly listening—about his cases. He'd told me I was a good sounding board, that I could see around corners he couldn't. Those were some of my favorite times.

"I wish you were here," I said to the air.

I imagined him across the table, smiling at me. Then I imagined myself talking to him about the murder at the bookshop. "What are we going to do about Page?"

I could see him frowning at me. "*We* are not going to do anything. Leave it to the professionals, El."

"Nolan has her pegged as his prime and only suspect. She didn't do it. You know her. She couldn't have done it even if she'd wanted to."

"I know. But Nolan's got to go by the book because of his relationship to our family. He can't look as if he's giving her a break. He'll make sure she's okay."

I twirled my mug in tight circles on the table. "I'm not so sure."

He tutted. "I never got why you didn't like him. He's been my best friend since fifth grade."

I lifted a shoulder, then let it drop. "He wasn't you. And he wanted to be."

In my mind, Harlan laughed his big, belly-shaking laugh. "Why would you think that?"

I couldn't explain the unsubstantiated feeling I'd had from the day I met Nolan. As if there had been some unnamed competition between them, and Nolan had found himself on the losing end far too many times. He was Harlan-lite. "I can't leave it up to him."

"If you get involved, you could make things worse for Page."

I leaned my head toward my shoulder. "Would you have brought her in?"

He gave one sharp nod. "I'd have had to."

Just like he'd brought Cammy in for questioning a few Halloweens ago.

"If you were going to prove her innocence," I asked, "what would you do?"

He gave me a thoughtful look, his hand reaching for mine across the table. "I'd look at the evidence beneath the evidence."

"What does that mean?"

Before he could answer, a shuffling noise came from the hallway and the illusion of Harlan in his chair vanished.

Page scuffed into the kitchen, hair a rat's nest around her head. She wore my robe and my slippers and yesterday's crazy heart sweater.

Stella padded in right behind her, did a down dog, then an up dog, then stared at me until I opened the back door to let her out.

Page spotted the mug of coffee across from me. "How did you know I was getting up?"

"I didn't."

"Oh." She sank into the chair, took a slug, and made a face. "How long has it been sitting here?"

I shrugged.

She sighed, got up and poured herself a fresh, hot cup with enough sugar to make a dentist ecstatic. "I've told you about how my mother died."

I nodded and drank some cold coffee. "Coming back from spending a weekend in New York with her best friend. On the way home, the bus blew a tire, then flipped down an embankment and eleven people died, including your mother."

She got up again and rummaged around the counter until she found a container of muffins. She offered me one. I shook my head. She sat again and peeled the muffin cup from the muffin as if the action required all of her concentration. "I was eleven. Dad died six months later."

Harlan had been twenty-one, just starting his career as a cop. We'd met a year later. Page had lived with him, then with us, until she was eighteen.

"The doctors said Dad died of a heart attack." Page pinched off a piece of muffin. "But, really, it was a broken heart."

"You were a kid. Of course you romanticize your parents' relationship." I'd heard about the magical love between Rose and Harry Hamlin, the kind of love they wrote stories about—the kind of stories Page liked to read even though her shop specialized in mysteries.

She let go of the muffin and dusted the crumbs from her fingertips. "No, it was more than that. My mom, she was like a sun. She lit up any room she walked into. And my dad, he was drawn in by her magnetic pull like he was an unlit candle and she was the only thing that could light him up."

"You're mixing your metaphors."

"You're missing the point."

"Which is?"

"Mom and Dad, they loved each other like you and Harlan did. Deep and strong. A once-in-a-lifetime, real kind of love. That's rare, Ellie."

Meeting him had been like finding a missing part of myself. He'd brought out the best in me. I hoped I'd done the same for him. And since he'd died, a huge hole had gaped open in my chest raw and bloody, and it just wouldn't close.

"Dad, he was never the same after Mom died. It was like the light had gone out of him. It never came back on. I don't want that for you." Tears pooled in her eyes. "I don't want you dying of a broken heart. I need you."

I didn't want to die, but I wasn't sure how to go on without him. "I can't just get over losing him" –I snapped my fingers— "like that."

She frowned, gaze imploring me. "But you can't let losing him mean you lose you, too."

Who was I without him? What was I supposed to do now that all our retirement plans were dashed? How was I supposed to fill a future where we'd been together and I was now alone?

I pushed away the mug of coffee. Those questions were too big to answer now. I had to concentrate on the problem at hand. "Then let's channel him and see how we can save you from a life in prison."

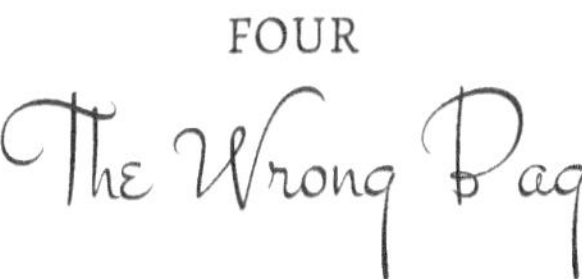

FOUR

I insisted on going to work with Page, only to find that the bookshop was still closed due to the investigation. Not knowing what we'd find, I'd left Stella at home with a lick mat and the television on for company.

"We can't sit around doing nothing." I paced the sidewalk outside the bookshop where crime-scene tape flapped in the breeze. Bright sun turned yesterday's snowfall into glitter, softening the icy crust on the sidewalk into slush. The cold, crisp air smelled like freshly ironed shirts and bit at my cheeks. "Not while Nolan is in there trying to find evidence against you."

"I didn't do it." She stamped one mukluked foot for emphasis, splashing slush against my jeans leg.

I shook my leg to dislodge the slush. "Of course not! Which is why we need to figure out who did."

I pulled on the sleeve of her purple coat, leading her up Main Street.

We walked over to the Brightside Bakery only to find it closed. Something I should have known by now. The bakery was always closed on Sundays and Mondays. And today was only Sunday, though it felt as if an eternity had gone by since yesterday.

We trekked over to Delta's Diner across the street. Inside, the air was redolent with the scent of toasted bread and bacon grease, which made my stomach gurgle with anticipation even though I had no appetite. We sat at a back booth with clichéd red vinyl benches—a booth from which I could still see everything that was happening outside the window and anyone who came in through the door—and ordered the Bright Morning eggs-hashbrown-bacon combo and coffee we didn't need.

Two white ceramic mugs thunked on the table, sloshing brown liquid onto the wooden surface. The waitress grunted and left before I could ask for cream. I pulled out a notepad from my bag and wrote "Suspects" at the top.

"Think, Page, who could have possibly wanted Kady dead?"

Page sucked in a breath and held it, shaking her head. "I have no idea. She seemed well liked by everyone who came in. Even some of the nastier customers were nice to her because they knew she was Gayle's daughter." Page snorted. "And nobody wants to get on Gayle's bad side."

I had a hard time believing any mother could hurt her own child, but given the domestic crimes spewed all over the news on a daily basis, how could I not at least consider that the good doctor had gotten rid of a problem daughter? My pen hesitated over the paper. Would she have taken the time to pose her daughter that way? It seemed too intimate. On the other hand, what was more intimate than a mother-and-daughter relationship? I just couldn't make myself put her mother on the first line.

"What do you know about her personal life?" I asked.

Page sat up taller as if I'd insulted her. "You know I'm not a meddler."

"Since when?"

A bowl of cream pods landed on the table. I added cream to my coffee, hoping it would tame the caffeine.

"She did have a boyfriend, and it seemed as if things weren't going well." Page leaned forward and whispered, "He came in a few times last week, and they had hush-hush conversations that seemed heated."

"How heated?"

"Well, I'm not one to pry..."

I rolled my eyes.

"...but I couldn't help overhearing. August-dog-days heated."

"Did you happen to overhear the topic?"

Page added what looked like half a dozen sugar packets to her coffee. "Gayle, of course."

"Mama dearest didn't approve of the boyfriend?"

"Not by a long shot. He definitely isn't country club material." Her spoon clinked against the side of her mug.

"What does he do?"

"Paints houses so he can afford to paint canvases. And as much as I believe in true love, I got the feeling he saw Kady as his ticket to being a full-time artist."

"What do you mean?"

She glanced around the diner as if to make sure nobody could hear our conversation. "There's a rumor that Kady would have gotten access to a cushy trust fund on her twenty-fifth birthday."

Harlan used to say that lust, loathing and loot were the big three motives in most crimes. "Which would've been?"

Page practically hissed. "April."

Two months from now. "Wouldn't he have kept her alive until she got her hands on the loot?"

"You'd think."

I poised my pen over the pad. "Do you know his name?"

"Erik Messer."

I'd seen the white van with the paint can spilling the

name Messer & Messer and the tag line "for all your painting needs" around town. "Jason's son?"

She nodded.

Knowing Jason, a stocky man with a definite blue collar, he probably wasn't too happy that his son wanted to follow a different kind of painting career. Unhappy enough to get rid of someone he saw as a problem?

"Okay, let's take another tack then." I didn't need any more coffee but drank it anyway. "Who did she see regularly during a workday?"

Page added cream to her coffee. "Most of the supplies arrive via UPS except for the coffee. That comes directly from Stoneley Coffee Roastery. They have a van that makes local deliveries. Nate usually comes once a week. The rest I get from Shaw's."

"Does Nate have a last name?"

"Leblanc."

I wrote "Nate Leblanc, coffee delivery" in the notebook. "How did he get along with Kady?"

"They seemed cordial enough. Nate's a chatterbox and tended to talk her ear off. She always had a treat for him."

To curb the chatter? Or because she liked him? "Did he have a crush on her?"

"I've only met him a couple of times, so it's hard to say."

"Okay, we'll have to talk to him next time he comes in. Who else?"

Page licked her spoon before putting it down on the bare tabletop. "Dave, the UPS guy, comes just about every day, either for the bookshop or for the café. And no, I don't know his last name."

I added "Dave, the UPS guy" to the list. "What was their relationship like?"

"I'm not sure she knew him at all. He left everything at the front desk. I could never get him to separate the packages."

Page turned her spoon over and over again against the tabletop, making an annoying *clink-clink* sound. "I hired Janelle Dewitt part time for the bookstore. You know, Diana's daughter. Mostly for weekends."

Another one of Page's charity cases. Janelle needed the job more than Page needed the help. And with her negative attitude, I could easily see her getting angry and bashing Kady on the head with a rolling pin. "How did she and Kady get along?"

"Fine, as far as I could tell. Janelle didn't really go to the café side unless she wanted coffee."

Didn't mean there hadn't been some sort of animosity between them. "Who else?"

"Kady wanted me to hire her a part-time dishwasher. Dylan Haney comes after school and works for a couple of hours." She smiled. "I think he has a little crush on her. He likes to make her laugh and comes in with a new joke every shift."

A crush made a good motive, especially if it wasn't reciprocated.

"That's it for staff." Page stared at the kitchen entrance. "What's taking them so long?"

"It's pretty busy."

Page looked around as if only now noticing the filled tables, the buzz of conversations all around us and the sideways glances as if the diners were all discussing the murder at the bookshop. The Brighton gossip mill wasn't going to help Page.

"Did she have problems with any of the regular customers?" I asked.

"I can't think of anyone who'd kill over a muffin."

"Yet here we are, trying to keep you out of prison."

Page waved a hand at me. *"Pfft!* Don't be so dramatic!"

"You're right, that's usually your thing."

She put a hand on her chest and an insulted look on her face. "Me? Dramatic?"

I lifted my brows and ran a look down her outfit. "Says the woman wearing a red tulle skirt with embroidered black hearts, a sweater with gnomes that spell "LOVE," fuzzy heart socks, and a headband with conversation hearts and rhinestones. Where did you even find that at my house?"

"I pulled a few things from the girls' closet." She patted the side of her headband. "What's wrong with a little fun, especially on holidays?"

I took in a long breath. She was right. Page was being Page. And that was what her customers expected. "Nothing."

Plates plunked down in front of us, trapping my notebook. Page's face brightened at the arrival of her breakfast. She tucked into her hashbrowns, then pointed her fork at her plate. "These are soooo good."

"Focus, Page. Who else?"

I glanced down at our pitiful list of suspects. Nobody seemed to truly have had a grudge against Kady. Or a motive. Dave, the UPS guy, was ancient. He did lift boxes for a living, though, so he could have thrown the body into the dumpster. Something I couldn't see tiny Janelle doing. She could barely lift a box of books.

I supposed unrequited love from Nate, the coffee delivery guy, or Dylan, the dishwasher, could have led to a crime of passion and opportunity.

"I can't think of anyone else." Page picked up a strip of bacon and bit into it, sending crumbles all over her eggs.

I picked at my scrambled eggs.

The staging had been so precise.

The white flour. The red hearts confetti. The choco-late-covered coffee beans.

That pointed to a close relationship, which brought me back to Erik.

But something niggled.

I tried the toast. Maybe that would settle my stomach.

Coffee beans... A zing raced through my mind. Coffee beans. A delivery guy with a crush. That put Nate in the number one spot. I circled his name. "We definitely need to talk to Nate."

"We're on the Monday delivery schedule." Page's phone rang. She riffled through her coat pockets and ulti-mately found it in her skirt pocket. "It's Nolan," she said, and answered. "Okay, thanks."

"What did he want?"

"He said I could go back into the shop."

"Let's go check if they found Kady's things."

***

THE MESS INSIDE THE CAFÉ'S KITCHEN distracted us from our goal of finding Kady's belongings. If she'd been murdered here, then her coat and purse should've been here. But to get to the bins, we'd have to clear a path.

Page turned around in the center of the kitchen with a

manic twirl that left me dizzy. "Why did they have to make such a mess?"

The counters and prep table were covered with kitchen utensils. Bins and containers had their covers askew, their contents spilled.

"They didn't want to miss anything?" I said, and thought Nolan should've ensured they'd been more delicate.

Page went to a white bin on rollers and pulled the cover up all the way. "Nothing there. Either the cops found her stuff, or it was never there."

"That's too bad." I pulled a garbage bag from the roll at one end of the prep table. The feel of it in my hand brought up a vague memory. "Are these the bags you always use?"

"Compostable." She toggled her head from side to side. "They're not so sturdy, but at least they don't last a lifetime in the landfill."

"These are green."

Page's eyes went wide as if she thought I was a little addled. "I can see that."

"Page, the bag covering Kady was black." I held up the compostable bag and shook it, making a hissing noise. Black like the kind contractors—or painters—used. "This is the wrong bag."

FIVE

Crumbs and Clues

age stared at the green garbage bag as if it were an alien. She plopped down on a stool in front of the prep table in the café's kitchen, gaze imploring me. "That proves I didn't do it, right?"

Not really, but maybe it would add a tablespoon of doubt to Nolan's cupful of circumstantial evidence.

"Stay here," I told Page, then gathered my coat, my bag, which held my notes, and the green garbage bag.

"Where are you going?"

"To ask Nolan what he knows."

Page bounced up. "I'll go with you."

"I don't want to walk you into a possible holding-on-suspicion situation. If he doesn't see you, he can't hold you, or question you, or put you in jail."

Page plopped back down on the stool. "When you put it that way…"

Bag in hand, holding my coat closed with the other hand rather than taking the time to zip it, I hiked across the slushy square to the police station inside Town Hall. I bypassed Norma Loomis, the ancient assistant with the cat's-eye glasses on a chain and silver bob that looked like a helmet. She managed the station with an iron fist.

"Hey, you can't go in there!" By the time Norma weeble-wobbled up from her creaky chair, I was already bursting through Harlan's—Nolan's—office door. "I need to know what you know."

He leaned in his chair as if the force of my entrance had shoved him backward. "You know I can't talk about an ongoing investigation."

He made a show of closing the file on his desk. The tab read "Katharine Dawn Chilton."

"How did Kady die?" I sat down in the uncomfortable metal chair in front of the desk without waiting for permission.

"Autopsy's not done yet."

I nodded and kept nodding as if that would help me come up with my next question. I should've taken the time to formulate a plan before rushing into his office. The whole world was topsy-turvy: I was the impulsive one, and Page was the sensible one.

"Could I have a glass of water?" I needed a minute to collect my scattered thoughts. And I would never get a look at that file unless he was somewhere else.

He studied me for a long moment, then gave a sharp nod. He slipped the file into the middle drawer of the desk, then got up.

As fast as I could, I opened the drawer and the file, snapped photos of everything, then returned the whole just as I'd found it.

By the time he returned with a paper cup of water, I'd sat back down, plucked a tissue from the box on the corner of the desk and blotted at fake tears.

"Thanks." I took the cup and drank a deliberate sip.

My gaze made a slow circle of the room that still held so much of Harlan—the Brighton Village map on the wall with notes in his handwriting, the corkboard tacked with reminder cards, BOLOs and photos of wanted criminals. Even the "Best Dad" mug the kids had given him years ago still stood above the blotter on the desk. I snatched it and dropped it in my bag. *Not yours*.

This time, the tears I dabbed were real. "How can you work here every day?"

He took his time folding his body back into the too-small chair. "Keeps him close."

"About Page..."

"It's not looking good."

"But it's all too" –I waved a hand in the air like a vortex as if that would help me catch the right word—"finger-pointy."

He raised his eyebrows, and the hint of a smile curved his lips. "Finger pointy?"

I groaned; I was even speaking like Page. I willed him to understand how wrong he was. "It's obvious someone planted all those pieces of 'evidence.' Someone wanted you to conclude that Page killed Kady."

"Sometimes the obvious is the truth."

"And sometimes it's a ruse."

"Ellie—"

"No, listen." I enumerated his so-called evidence on my fingers. "Page doesn't bake. The rolling pin isn't hers—"

"A crime of passion using what's at hand."

"So, you think Kady was killed in the kitchen."

"Ellie..."

"Fine." I narrowed my gaze at him, moving on to the next finger. "Page isn't used to wearing reading glasses yet, so she keeps losing them. There're at least a dozen pairs floating around the shop. Anyone could have grabbed one and planted it."

He crossed his arms over his chest. "Or the glasses could have fallen off her head and the keys from her pocket when she dumped the body."

I threw a hand up. "There you go. Page isn't strong enough to lift the deadweight of a woman above her head and into the dumpster."

"Rage gives people superhuman strength."

"What about the keys?" I fisted my hand, wanting to jar something loose in his rusted brain. "They could've been anybody's."

"With a purple bat fob?"

Shoot. The leather fob was one of a kind, made especially for Page. "Someone could have stolen them from under the shop counter where she keeps them when she's working." I shook a finger at him, remembering something. "She had them on Saturday morning. I saw her use them to open the shop. The little bat was flopping around as she twisted the key. There's no way she killed Kady with a store filled with customers."

"It happened quickly."

I blew a raspberry. "Not that quickly. Not with the staging. And half the town can vouch that Page never left the counter on Saturday."

He sighed, a deep, put-upon sigh. "Listen—"

"No, you listen." I jabbed the metal desktop with a finger, emphasizing every word. "If it's such a crime of passion, then where did the black garbage bag come from?" I pulled the green garbage bag from the bookshop out of my bag. "Page uses green compostable bags. *That's* what she would've had at hand."

He leaned his head toward a shoulder and let out a frustrated breath. "Can you trust me for just a little while?"

"Page's life is at stake."

His eerie golden gaze speared mine. "What would Harlan do?"

I flicked a hand toward his desk drawer. "He wouldn't take planted evidence at face value. He'd keep digging until he found the truth—the *real* truth."

"That's what I intend to do."

Although I gave him a nod, there was no way in hell I was trusting Page's freedom to his intention. "What was on the note?"

"What note?"

"I saw the crime scene team put pieces of paper in an evidence bag."

He got up and opened the door—an invitation to leave. "You have to let me do my job, Ellie, and not interfere."

That was a promise I couldn't keep.

When I returned to the bookshop, Page waited by the door and all but jumped on me as I walked in.

"What happened?" Her hands gripped my arm, and her eyes shone with hope. "What did he say?"

I hated giving her bad news, but I wasn't going to sugarcoat her situation. "It's up to us to find the truth."

The hope vanished, making her face droop. "Where do we start?"

"At the source."

Page lifted an eyebrow in question.

"The mother."

"Okay, let's go." Page headed around the counter to grab her backpack purse.

Before we could make an exit, the bell above the bookshop door rattled. Bailey walked in tentatively as if she weren't sure she was welcome here. In her olive-green puffy coat and olive-green hat, she looked like a marshmallow left at the back of a cupboard for years.

"Sorry to bother you," she said, coming over to the counter. "But in all the commotion yesterday, I forgot to have you sign my time sheet." She reached into a well-worn brown leather satchel and pulled out a folded sheet of paper. She unfolded it on the counter and ironed it flat with the side of her hand.

"Right." Page grabbed a pen and scribbled her name

with a flourish. "I'm looking for someone to bake and manage the café. Are you interested?"

Bailey took the time sheet from Page, folded it again and put it back in her bag with careful, deliberate movements as if she were afraid to stir up a mad dog.

"Uh." She turned her head toward the café's dark kitchen, a deep frown pinching her forehead. "I don't think so. Someone died in that kitchen, and nobody's been arrested yet. I don't want to end up like her."

"No worries." Page came around the bookshop counter, hooked an arm through Bailey's and led her toward the café. "We'll make sure someone's always here, so you won't ever have to work alone. How does that sound?"

"I don't know…" Bailey's feet dragged and she looked about to bolt.

"Try it." Page turned on the lights in the kitchen, illuminating all the shiny surfaces and their unlimited possibilities. The place still held on to the faint odor of lemon dish soap and piney floor cleaner. "For a day. See how you feel."

"I—uh."

"Aren't you tired of working temp jobs? Isn't a steady job where you have creative freedom something you've been looking for?"

"Yes, but—"

Page tutted. "Kady was a troubled girl. Are you troubled, Bailey?"

"Not really."

"Then why would anyone want to kill you?"

"I'd feel more comfortable if her killer was in jail."

Page gave Bailey's arm a no-worries pat. "The best and the brightest are on the job. It won't be long before they have someone behind bars. And like I said, you won't be alone. From now on, we work in pairs or not at all."

"I suppose—"

"Great! Then it's settled. Can you start now?"

Bailey's gaze darted around the kitchen as if the killer were hiding behind a bin and would pop out at any moment. "I guess."

"Great!" Page slid a 3-inch, white binder off the shelf and plunked it on the stainless steel table. She rippled the plastic-protected pages. "These are the recipes Kady's been using. We have certain staples the customers expect—the sunrise muffins, the browned-butter chocolate chip cookies and the lemon bars. But you can fill the bakery case with whatever else you want. At least two kinds of muffins in the morning. Two kinds of cookies and bars for lunch. Try to have at least one gluten-free option. Cupcakes for the afternoon."

"Sounds easy enough."

Page glanced around the kitchen as if looking for something. "You already know how everything works."

"I guess."

"Okay." She grabbed a white bakery box and filled it with muffins, then turned to me. "Let's go."

"You just promised Bailey she wouldn't have to work alone in the shop."

"She's not alone. I called Janelle and just heard her come in." When she reached the arch that separated the café from the bookshop, Page put a hand around the side of her mouth and yelled, "Janelle! You're in charge of the counter!"

A mousy "Okay" came from the back room.

"See," Page said to me, grinning like a fool. As she headed for the door, she juggled her coat, backpack and bakery box. "All good. Let's go."

SIX

Recipe for Trouble

Page drove us to Chapel Hill. The white Georgian mansion with its black shutters made an imposing impression, sitting atop a hill at the end of a half-mile-long driveway, as if judging each arrival for worthiness. The bones of sculpted gardens—hedges, trellises, arbors, pergolas and gazebos—hid under the cover of snow. The horseshoe drive almost made me wish we'd arrived by horse carriage.

"Some place," I said, gaping at the house.

"It's been in the Chilton family forever." Page parked by the main entrance, fronted by a portico, stopping so abruptly I had to brace my hands on the dashboard to avoid bashing my head on the windshield. "They used to have a guard dog and, when we were kids, we'd play dare." She sniggered. "I never got caught."

"Let me guess. You brought dog treats."

"Hamburger."

I shook my head. "No wonder Harlan was always so worried about you."

She pooh-poohed the thought with a hand and returned her gaze to the house. "I wonder who'll inherit it now that Kady's gone."

Page turned off the ignition and looked at me. "So, what's the plan?"

"I thought you had one, the way you were driving like a bat out of hell."

"I just want this over, you know."

I understood. "We need to see if Gayle will let us look at Kady's place."

I just wish I could skip the condolences part; it hit too close to home. From experience, I knew it only made the pain worse, freshening it just when you thought you were finally starting to form a scab. And yet, they were expected.

"The cops have probably been through the place." Page clucked her tongue as if she were missing out on something.

"Doesn't mean they saw all there is to see." Given Nolan's insistence on believing planted evidence, unless something pointed to Page, it probably hadn't been collected and bagged.

"True." Page nodded and grabbed her backpack and

the bakery box. "Food is always a good conversation opener."

I couldn't argue with that. At the door, I rang the doorbell. It echoed in a series of bongs deep into the cavernous house. My mind couldn't help going back to that awful morning when I'd opened the door to find the whole police department on my stoop. Now that I was on this side of the door, I could see that the visit had been just as hard for them. The waiting. The dread of having to deliver the most awful of news, or the impart of condolences. I took in a long breath, willing the knot in my chest to loosen.

Eventually, Gayle opened the door. The usually perfectly postured Gayle seemed stooped and brittle. Her face, usually an expression of certainty, had taken on an ashen quality. Her usually perfectly coiffed hair looked as if it hadn't seen a brush today. When who we were registered, she narrowed her gaze at Page. "What makes you think you're welcome here?"

"I came to offer my condolences." Page presented Gayle with the bakery box.

My condolences refused to climb out of my throat and I opened my mouth like a fish on shore.

Gayle's hand gripped the door as if she meant to slam it in Page's face. "You were supposed to keep her safe."

Page took a half step back. "From what?"

"From herself! This job was supposed to give her structure, purpose, until she came to her senses." Gayle waved the bakery box away. "That will clog your arteries."

"Kady baked them," Page said.

I elbowed her. I'd baked those muffins, and Page knew it. What was she doing?

Gayle's face tightened with anguish. Her eyes grew shiny with tears. She cleared her throat, took the box and hugged it to her chest. "Thank you."

"I thought you were all for Kady baking," Page said. "That's why you made me hire her."

Gayle's breath ratcheted as if her lungs had steps and climbing each was an ordeal. "Kady didn't know what she wanted. She was dabbling. And I knew that if I made her buckle down to her responsibilities too early, she would rebel. I figured in a year or two, she'd be ready."

"Responsibilities?" I asked.

Gayle's gaze skirted around the entry hall that was almost as big as my whole house. "She's a Chilton. Was a Chilton. The house, the grounds, the Chilton Foundation, they were all her inheritance. Her family's history and future rested in her care."

That was a heavy load of expectations. Heavy enough to warrant filicide? Except that Gayle looked genuinely grief-stricken.

"And now, what happens?" I asked as gently as I could.

Gayle shook her head in slow arcs. "With Ernest gone and Kady gone, I'm not sure. I certainly have no interest in the place."

Ernest Chilton had been a prominent businessman in the area. His family had made their fortune during the early days of the railroad, then kept one step ahead of ever-changing technology, from cars to private planes and all the support systems that went with it. As a matter of fact, the Chiltons owned the local general aviation airport. Was Gayle angry that she'd now have to take over the family business as well as run her own?

But the Chiltons and their future, or lack thereof, wasn't why we'd come here. We needed evidence that someone other than Page had murdered Kady.

"Is there any way we could see Kady's living quarters?" I asked.

"What on earth for?" Gayle's face turned formidable as if she were ready to stand over her dead child and protect her body.

Considering she'd all but blamed Page for her daughter's death, I couldn't use Page's freedom as an excuse. And given that she was mourning her daughter, she probably wasn't up on the gossip—yet. "We want to make sure Kady's killer is caught."

With extreme care, she placed the bakery box on the

table, then turned to face us, arms under her chest. "That's why we have a police department, isn't it?"

"Yes, well, the investigation team isn't local, and they don't understand how a place like Brighton works."

She huffed. "And you do?"

Even though I'd lived in Brighton for almost thirty years, I was still considered an outsider.

Page tsked. "Ellie solved a ten-year-old cold case a few Halloweens ago when the police couldn't."

Gayle examined me as if I were a wonky EKG. "I don't suppose an extra set of eyes will harm the situation." She speared Page with a sharp look. "Someone needs to pay for what happened to Kady."

Gayle grabbed a coat from the closet behind the front door and a key from a glass bowl on the table. She led us through the center hallway arch, into a kitchen that looked both old-fashioned and modern and was big enough to cater a ball, then out the kitchen door. The place smelled of age, wood polish, and old money. She took a shoveled flagstone garden path to a small—by comparison—building on the far side of the gardens.

"Do you have any idea who would've wanted to hurt Kady?" I asked as we walked.

"As I told the police, the only person that comes to mind is Erik Messer." Her voice held enough acid to eat through stone. No love lost there. "She'd broken up with him, and he wasn't taking it well." Gayle huffed. "The gravy train was over, and he wanted it to go on."

"Gravy train?" Page asked, so busy gawping at all the garden structures that she almost ran into Gayle.

"Kady—against my advice—paid for all his art supplies and gave him space in the carriage house attic to work."

Statistics agreed with her. I thought of Harlan, responding to that domestic call when it had been way too early for someone to already be drunk. Another boyfriend who hadn't been able take no and had chosen to destroy rather than walk away.

My throat constricted. I wasn't going to cry. Not in public.

Gayle unlocked the carriage house door and opened it. "Please be respectful of her belongings."

"Of course," I said, hands deep in my coat pockets. "We won't be long."

Gayle gave a sharp nod. A painful crease grooved her forehead, and she backed away from the door. I got that. I hadn't been able even open the door to Harlan's office until this morning. She'd had only had a day.

"Come by the house when you're done," she said, "so I know to lock up."

"We will," I said. "Thank you."

I closed the door behind us.

"I don't think she did it." Page dropped her backpack, her scarf and hat.

My gaze circled the neat area. "What makes you say that?"

"She wouldn't have let us in here if she did."

"Kady wasn't killed here. Nolan thinks she was attacked in the café's kitchen." Not that he'd come out and actually said it, but he had implied it. "But I don't think so, either."

"What are we looking for?" Page asked, turning in circles in the middle of the open-concept room. An L formed the living room and kitchen. The bedroom was through the door at the square, filling the L.

"Anything that could point to someone having a reason to have killed Kady."

"That is awfully vague."

"You'll know it when you see it." I hoped so. "Let's divide and conquer. You take the living room. I'll take the bedroom. Whoever's finished first can look through the kitchen."

Kady's bedroom was surprisingly spartan. A white iron bed with a light-blue daisy medallion comforter, a pile of pillows—some with blue-and-white stripes, others with shams of the same medallion pattern—a white dresser topped with a mirror and nothing else on the surface, and a white rocking chair. Her closet was neatly organized by type and color and contained only clothes and shoes. I riffled through the dresser drawers, looking for a diary or a box where she might have kept her secrets. I tried under the mattress and under the bed. Nothing. I looked for a loose floorboard under the area rug and in the closet. No luck.

"Did you find anything?" I asked Page as I stepped into the living room. The gray couch and lounge chair looked secondhand. Her bookcase, with its built-in desk, was as neat as her bedroom.

"Just this photo album." Page sat at the end of the couch, leafing through the photo book, the bound kind you could get at a pharmacy photo counter.

"Looks like she was still friends with a couple of her classmates—Samantha Garvey and Ashley Alexander."

"Something to look into." I mentally added them to our list.

"Most of the photos are of her or the boyfriend or them together."

"Take pictures of the pictures."

"Already done." She closed the book. "They look like they're in love."

"Until one of them gets drunk and kills the other." Yep, I'd become a cynic since last year.

I headed toward the kitchen. This room was the only one stamped with Kady's personality. It smelled of butter and sugar and chocolate. Gayle might have thought that baking had been a passing fancy for her daughter, but the neatly organized cookbooks, the lovingly placed equipment and the shelves filled with quality ingredients told me that Gayle was in denial. Baking, by all appearances, meant the world to Kady.

In between the cookbooks, I spied a 9 x 12-inch navy hardcover sketchbook. The pages were unlined and filled with photos of baked goods, drawings of baked goods and squiggle lines of notes around each. Some pages had what looked like experiments with measurements and ingredients crossed out and refined, then a few pages later, the final recipe appeared on a clean page.

"What do you make of this?" I asked Page, walking the sketchbook over to the living room.

Page leafed through the book, then stopped at a page, her finger tracing the treat. "Huh. That looks like one of Dani Saunders's apple cider donuts."

I gawked over Page's shoulder. It did look like Dani's famous donuts. I turned a few more pages. Then what I was seeing dawned on me. "Kady was reverse-engineering recipes. Look, that's Maeve Carpenter's hand pies, and Marissa Marchetti's chocolate love cake! I'll bet you those finished recipes are her versions of those treats." My mind spun with possibilities. "Did Kady use any of these recipes at the café?"

"I don't know." Page frowned. "We'll have to check the bake book when we get back to the shop."

I looked around the room. "I think we're done here."

Page lifted her head to stare at the ceiling. "Gayle mentioned Erik used the attic."

I slipped the sketchbook into my bag.

"What are you doing?" Page asked, all but hissing. "You can't take it."

"How else are we going to figure out if this is the reason she was killed?"

"You don't really think someone killed her over a donut or a cake, do you?"

I arranged the cookbooks on the shelf to hide the space created by the missing sketchbook. To the police, this book would appear like nothing more than baking notes. Nothing of importance.

But what if Kady had used one of these reverse-engineered recipes at the café? What if the originator had found out? "Someone stealing a recipe could be a motive for murder."

THE ATTIC HAD BEEN SWEPT CLEAN. NOTHING OF Erik remained except dabs of paint on the wooden floorboards. We'd found no hidden nook or diary or treasure box. Only a few spider webs. Had Gayle gotten rid of the evidence of the unwanted boyfriend, or had Kady cleaned house after breaking up with her boyfriend? I'd meant to ask Gayle when we returned to the main house, but she'd shown us to the door before I could ask anything.

Once back at the bookshop, crawling with customers browsing books and buying baked goods, we headed straight for the kitchen and the binder with the recipes Kady had baked for the café. The kitchen smelled of cinnamon and sugar, wafting from the bakery rack, which was filled with sweet rolls, and of coffee, steaming from the blasted machine. My stomach gurgled. I'd barely touched my breakfast this morning and we'd skipped lunch altogether.

Page thwacked the binder on the stainless steel table and opened the cover, revealing the first recipe. We leafed through the pages, comparing them to the sketchbook, but couldn't find any of the recipes in her sketchbook in the binder.

Page dropped onto a stool and reached for a cinnamon roll. "Told you no one would kill over a muffin."

"Looks like a dead end." I sighed. I'd been so sure this would be the clue that would crack the case wide open.

Bailey rushed through the kitchen door, an empty platter in hand, a big smile taking up her face. "The cinnamon rolls have been flying off the shelf."

She frowned at the sight of the bakery binder. "What are you looking for?"

"Apparently, a ghost." Page juggled the roll as she returned the binder to its place on the shelf.

Bailey's eyebrows rose. "A ghost?"

"We thought someone might have killed Kady over a recipe." I reached for a cinnamon roll and bit into it, teeth sinking into the air-soft pastry. "These are really good, Bailey."

"Thanks. I've been perfecting this recipe for years." She glanced at Page, a worried look creasing her eyes. "I hope you don't mind."

"I told you," Page said around a mouthful of roll. "You have creative control as long as the regulars are happy." She lifted the roll. "Especially if the results are this good."

Her smile rose again. "Thanks." She nodded toward the binder. "Were you looking for a specific recipe? I studied them between customers."

"No." I licked vanilla icing from my fingers, disappointment plunging down to my stomach. "It was just a hunch that proved wrong."

SEVEN

Red Scarves and Red Herrings

On Monday, Page and I got to the shop by six thirty to catch Nate, the coffee delivery guy. According to Kady's records, that was the time he usually made his stop. When the sound of his van backing up in the alley filtered through the back kitchen door, Page nearly tripped over a stool, rushing to open it.

Nate reached into the van for a wooden crate filled with five-pound bags of coffee roasted at his family's business in Stoneley. His round face lit up with its usual friendliness. "Hey, Page."

"Nate," Her breath steamed like dragon fire in the cold air.

Nate carried the crate to the stainless steel prep table. "I heard about Kady."

"Horrible," Page said. Then, without preamble,

launched right into a question. "How well did you know her?"

I sighed. Subtlety wasn't Page's forte.

Nate blinked but recovered fast. "Not well. We chatted when I stopped in. That's all."

Page arched a brow so dramatically I was amazed it didn't lift her bangs. "About?"

He shrugged and unpacked the coffee, one bag at a time, slowly and methodically. "Pastry, coffee, life."

"That's pretty vague," Page said a little too brightly.

"Like I said—just a customer."

I stepped in. "When you made deliveries, that's the only time you saw her?"

"Yeah." His hands paused mid-unpacking. "Why?"

"Where were you on Thursday night?" Accusation curled under each of Page's words like a cat ready to pounce.

Nate's face tightened, his jaw ticking once. "Out of town."

Page folded her arms. "How convenient."

"Page—" I started.

He jabbed the last coffee bag down with so much force the bag crinkled down two inches. "Are you implying I had something to do with Kady's death?"

"I'm asking you." Page leaned in, voice low. "You liked her."

He stared at Page for a second too long. "She was a good listener. That's all. She always had some cookies for me." His hands wrapped around the crate's handles. "Thoughtful that way."

"What kind of cookies?" Page asked.

His mouth opened. Closed. "Does it matter?"

I placed a plate of cookies in front of him. "You're the reason she made the hazelnut shortbreads."

He flinched. "Look, she was a nice kid. Too young for me."

"You're what, mid-thirties?" I asked. An older man dating a much younger girl was acceptable in our society.

"I didn't kill her." He reached one hand into his coat pocket, fingers brushing against something in his pocket, then stopped, hesitated and grabbed the empty crate instead.

"Do you sell chocolate-covered coffee beans?" I asked.

"Just coffee. Beans or ground." He headed for the door.

As he reached to push open the door, Page called after him. "Did you ever see her cry?"

Nate froze midstep. His back went rigid. His voice, when it came, was too careful. "She wasn't the type. Always had a smile."

Then he stalked out the door without another word,

the door swinging shut behind him with a *thwack* of finality.

"Interesting comment from someone who claims not to have known her."

Page stared at the door, gaze narrowed. "She *was* the type. Especially lately."

"What do you mean?"

Page bit into one of the hazelnut shortbreads from the plate we'd prepared for Nate. "Since her breakup with Erik, every little suggestion, even if it wasn't a criticism, seemed to bring on the waterworks."

I nodded. "Nate didn't just notice her. He knew something about what was going on with her."

"That wasn't denial." Page stuffed the rest of the cookie in her mouth and chewed. "That was avoidance."

"I don't know what he's hiding." I said and reached for a cookie. "But it's personal. He's protecting something." I bit absently into the cookie. "Or someone."

———

AFTER PAGE FLIPPED THE CLOSED SIGN TO OPEN, I barely had time to tie on my apron before the bell above the shop's door rang. Bailey wasn't due for her shift until lunch because I had no intention of staying until closing. The Golden Girls book club trooped in with a flurry of floral perfume, clinking bracelets and strong opinions. A blast of frigid February air followed them in.

"Honestly, I thought I was going to break a hip on the sidewalk." Margo led the charge, bright-red faux-fur collar dusted with snow. "Black ice everywhere. Doesn't the town salt anymore?"

"I told you to wear boots with treads." Pearl flapped her mittened hands toward Margo's black leather knee-high boots with two-inch heels. "You insist on style over safety."

June blew into her cold hands. "It's a fashion risk I'm willing to take, too. Unlike Dorothy, who's still wearing those tragic moon boots from the '80s."

Dorothy adjusted her lavender rhinestone glasses. "And I'm the only one here who hasn't fallen this winter. So who's laughing now?"

I put on my brightest smile and reached for a notepad. "Morning, ladies. What can I get for you today?"

"You're not ready for us?" Pearl tsked, peering over the counter. "Kady always had the kettle on and the coffee going before we got here. She *anticipated*."

"And she had the scones warming." June placed a baggie of lemon wedges on the counter as if claiming territory.

Dorothy sighed a mournful sigh. "Kady had a way. No offense, Ellie."

"None taken." I refrained from pointing out this wasn't my job, that I was just helping out Page. "We have raspberry scones today. I'll warm them up for you."

June looked around. "Don't tell me you're running the place on your own today?"

I tightened the apron string around my waist. "For now."

"One London Fog, one black coffee—none of that flavored nonsense—one extra-hot chai and one Earl Grey," Margo said, not even bothering to look at the menu. "Honey for Pearl's chai." She put a hand next to her mouth as if to impart a secret. "Kady always gave us an extra scone to share."

"Real cream for the coffee," Dorothy added. "The kind that makes your arteries sing."

"I'll get these drinks ready for you." I retreated to the dreaded coffee machine before they could ask for any more extras—like the lavender sugar Kady had in the back. "Your favorite table is waiting for you."

They made their way over to the table right in front of the window, unspooling scarves and trading opinions about the new triangular flags that hung from the street-lamp posts.

I filled mugs and plated scones. By the time I delivered the tray to their table, the Golden Girls were already deep into this month's book club pick: *Death Comes to the Garden Party*.

"I thought the vicar did it." June reached for a scone, tore it in half and slathered it with butter. "Anyone who bakes that many casseroles has something to hide."

"Don't be ridiculous." Pearl stirred honey in her chai. "The gardener, clearly. All that potting soil and no alibi."

Margo rolled her eyes. "Please. The only true villain was the editor who let that pacing drag in the second act."

Dorothy leaned in. "Speaking of drama, want to talk about what happened last Monday? Now that Kady's turned up dead, that scene in *this* café last Monday takes on new meaning, right?"

"The woman with the red scarf?" Pearl's eyebrows pinched together.

That grabbed up my attention, and I made excuses to stay at the counter and listen in on their conversation.

"Oh, yes." June tutted. "That scarf was long enough to lasso a cow. Cashmere, I'm sure of it. Bright red."

They talked over each other, arguing about whether the woman's coat had been brown or black, whether her hair had been brown or black, whether she'd worn lipstick or not.

June leaned in, voice low and dramatic. "She slammed her hand on the counter. I thought the glass was going to break."

"That woman had a nasty attitude, for sure. She nearly knocked over Pearl's tea on her way out." Dorothy swept an arm dramatically. "Didn't even apologize. Just swooped out like she was headed for the stage."

Margo frowned. "I don't remember seeing her before. And I'm good with faces."

Pearl lowered her voice. "She kind of looks like that cake lady. Also, she has the kind of face that makes her look like anybody's cousin."

"She seemed mad at something," Dorothy said, "but I couldn't hear what."

"I could." June tapped her hearing aid. "She said something like 'You always take what doesn't belong to you.' Or maybe it was 'You took it again.' One of those."

"That's not what I heard," Pearl said. "I thought she said, 'You don't get to do this twice.' Could've been about a man."

Margo shook her head. "Nah, Kady was with Erik forever. She loved that boy, and he was over the moon in love with her. That much was obvious." She sipped her London Fog as if it were whiskey. "Could've been about a parking spot for all we know."

"Or a coffee order gone wrong." Pearl grinned. "Kady *did* once mix up someone's oat milk with cream. That woman stormed out like she'd been poisoned."

I managed a smile as I gathered the empty plates and

used napkins onto a tray, my mind going over what they'd said. *You always take what doesn't belong to you*. That could mean anything, but it was definitely specific. Same with *You don't get to do this twice*. Do what?

"The woman was angry. I remember that." Margo wrapped the extra scone in a paper napkin and tucked it in her purse. "Didn't order anything. Just marched in here like she owned the place, said that nasty accusation to Kady and *boom*. Kady turned the color of those valentines hanging from the ceiling. Kady said something like 'You're wrong.'"

"The woman kind of smelled like cardamom." Dorothy frowned, as if trying to get back the olfactory memory.

"No, like Mojave Ghost." June nodded with certainty. They all stared at her. "What? My niece wears it. It's floral *and* woodsy. And lasts forever."

Tray in hand, I turned to leave, then paused. "None of you know her name?"

"Kady didn't introduce us." June shrugged. "And the woman didn't stay long."

"But you all remember the scarf."

Four gray heads bobbed in unison.

"Hard to forget," Margo said. "It was like a red flag billowing down the street."

Dorothy lifted her bejeweled phone. "The way she was carrying on, I was about to call 9-1-1."

Margo peered out the window. "We should go before the snow gets any worse."

They all rose as one, dropped bills on the table, gathered their coats, hats and mitts and left, letting in another wave of arctic air.

Back behind the counter, I placed the dishes in the dish tub for washing, my thoughts buzzing louder than that blasted coffee contraption. A woman in an expensive red scarf. A mysterious argument a week before Kady died. Were the two incidents related?

And a phrase that didn't make sense, given who Kady'd been—*You always take what doesn't belong to you.* She could have bought anything she'd wanted, or her mother could have. Even this job.

What couldn't she have gotten for herself or from her mother?

Erik, her boyfriend? The one her mother had said she'd broken up with. Was that the truth, or what Gayle wanted to believe? I needed to have a chat with him.

I glanced out the window at the snow swirling as if the woman with the red scarf would appear.

All I have to figure out, I thought, *is who owns a red scarf...and a grudge.*

EIGHT

Stirring the Pot

Dave, the UPS guy, showed up right on time at two and parked his truck at the front door with the practiced precision of someone who'd done this a thousand times.

"He's so regular," Page said, checking the heart-shaped watch that dangled from her wrist, "that you could set your watch by his arrival."

The bell above the door jangled, cold air spiraling in behind him, making me rub my arms to keep warm. Bundled in his brown uniform jacket, arms full of boxes stacked chin high, he stomped the snow from his boots onto the welcome mat.

He grunted. "Where do you want these?"

Page rolled her eyes. "Where do you *always* put them?"

He dumped the stack near the checkout counter and

straightened with a sigh, rubbing his gloved hand across his forehead. "Good day, ladies."

"Dave?" I came around the desk.

He hesitated, one boot half-turned toward the door. "Huh."

"Do you know Kady?"

His mouth flattened. "Kady who?"

"The baker," Page said. "The one who leaves brownies for you."

He glanced at the counter where the treat basket usually waited.

"I heard she died," he said, voice flat.

"Murdered," Page whispered. "Here. Over the weekend."

Dave blinked. "Wow. That's...something."

"Did you know her?" I asked again, watching him closely, noting the deep fatigue that lined his face.

His weight shifted from foot to foot. "Couldn't pick her out of a lineup to save my life." He hooked a thumb toward the door. "Anyway, I've got a tight schedule. Can't stand around all day chatting."

He turned to go, pulling the door open—but as he did, his gaze lingered for a moment on the empty treat basket.

"Shame," he said, almost to himself. "She made great brownies."

Then he stepped outside, letting the door jangle shut behind him.

We both went to the window and leaned forward to peer through the painted hearts, ribbons and cupids. He climbed into his truck and pulled away, the rumble of the engine climbing up the street.

Page turned to me, lifting an eyebrow. "Didn't know her, huh?"

"Maybe he just knew her baking."

"Or maybe he's not telling us everything." She pointed her chin toward the New Book shelf, where the spines of cozy mysteries glinted under heart-shaped fairy lights. "It's never the obvious person."

"I'm not ready to cross him off the list just yet."

I kept watching the truck's taillights and spotted Bailey's car parked on the street—an old Toyota that had more rust than paint and a passenger's side window of plastic sheeting. "Speaking of which, do you think Bailey could have killed Kady?"

"Why? They didn't know each other."

"Her arrival is awfully coincidental."

"I forgot to cancel with the temp agency. That order was in place weeks before Kady died. And *I* convinced Bailey to work here." Page swatted my arm. "Stop seeing guilt everywhere. Just because she drives an old car and lives in a trailer park doesn't mean she's a bad person."

I pushed away from the window. "I didn't say that."

"You tend to see the worst in people." Page returned to the checkout desk.

"I'm trying to keep you free."

"And I love you for it."

———

At the sound of the door opening, I looked up from the case notes I was studying, hoping something would jump out to give me direction. Dylan, the dishwasher Kady had hired to help her after school, slipped inside the bookshop, shoulders weighed down by a scuffed black backpack. Snowflakes clung to his shoulder straps and the hood of his sweatshirt. A sweatshirt, I noted, rather than a winter jacket.

The scent of books, coffee and cinnamon from the rolls Bailey was baking hung in the air, but he didn't glance toward the bakery or the book displays. Head down, he went straight toward the back room like a shadow trying not to get noticed.

From the corner table, hands wrapped around a half-finished mug of red chai, I watched him shuffle. Dylan avoided eye contact with everyone and barely acknowledged Page's hello.

Grief over Kady's death?

Page wrapped orders around books delivered earlier. "Hey, Dylan, the compost bin's full again. And the hot water's been fussy today. I've got someone coming in to fix it tomorrow. But for today, try to economize, okay?"

Dylan mumbled something that might have been "Okay" before disappearing into the back room.

I got up and went to the checkout counter where Page was working. "I need a few minutes with him."

"No, you don't." Page wore a "Don't-mess-with-me" expression I rarely saw.

"I'm not accusing him of anything," I said. "I just need to talk to him."

"He didn't kill Kady." Page snapped a rubber band around another book a little too hard, and it broke.

"I think he had feelings for her and something happened."

Page's gaze narrowed. "He's sixteen. And awkward. Having a crush doesn't make him dangerous."

I leaned in. "Teenagers' pre-frontal cortices aren't fully formed, and sometimes, that makes them impulsive."

Page jammed the book onto the bookcase behind her. "You have no idea what that kid's carrying."

"I'd like to find out."

"No." This firmness wasn't Page's style.

"If she rejected him—"

"Drop it, Ellie." Page's gaze flicked to the back room. "I know he didn't do it."

"You *think* you know. You've got a soft heart—"

"I *know*." The finality in her tone suggested that should've been the end of it, but I couldn't let it go. Why was she fighting me so hard about an interview that could help clear her name?

"Then a few questions won't hurt."

Before Page could respond, Dylan reappeared from the kitchen with a tub to gather dirty dishes from the café. When he saw us standing there, his steps slowed. Something like suspicion, or maybe guilt, rushed across his face, followed by the turtling of his neck into his shoulders— that instinct to shrink, to disappear.

"Dylan." I smiled at him. "Can we talk?"

He hooked a thumb over his shoulder. "I— I've got to get these cleaned up—"

"It won't take long." I took his elbow and led him to a café table.

His eyes went wild. "Did I do something wrong?"

"You liked Kady, didn't you?"

"I didn't—I couldn't have hurt her. I swear."

Page strode toward us. "That's enough, Ellie!"

I ignored Page and plowed on. Didn't she realize that her freedom was on the line if we couldn't figure out who'd killed Kady?

"I know you didn't hurt her," I said, gentling my voice. "This isn't an interrogation. I just want to understand."

Dylan gripped the dish tub hard.

Page jammed her fists onto her hips. "Ellie!"

"She was kind to you." I sat at a table and invited him to do so too, but he stayed standing. "Listened to you. Gave you treats. Noticed you."

His jaw worked like he wanted to say something but couldn't find the right words.

"It must've been hard to see her go out with someone else."

He flinched.

"Ellie, stop!" I'd never heard Page's voice so sharp.

"It wasn't that way!" The dish tub thunked onto the table. "She said it was fine."

Page and I both went still.

"What was fine?" I asked, as if I were tiptoeing through a minefield.

Dylan glanced from Page to me, his face pale, blotchy. "Nothing."

"Dylan," Page said, reaching for his hand. "Look at me."

He did, reluctantly, his eyes glistening with tears.

"You're not in trouble," Page said. "You don't have to answer her questions."

He opened his mouth, then shut it. A long silence

stretched. Then he collapsed onto a chair as if someone had taken his feet out from under him. "It's not stealing if it's going to waste."

Dylan kept going, as if he couldn't stop now. "It started with muffins. The ones no one bought and were too stale to sell the next day. Kady left them out, and she told me she was just going to throw them out. Then I started taking sandwiches, too. Just the ones no one claimed. Just...stuff that would get tossed. That's all."

His shoulders sagged and his floppy hair fell forward, hiding his face. "I'm sorry. I know it's wrong. But my sisters—"

"Were hungry." Page sat down too. "I get it."

"I really need this job." His forehead pleated. "Are you going to fire me?"

"Of course not." Page patted his arm. "You're not fired. You're fed."

Dylan blinked.

"You'll take leftovers home. Officially." Page glanced toward the kitchen, where Bailey baked with soft music in the background. "I'll make sure Bailey knows. No sneaking. No shame."

His mouth fell open. "Really?"

"Really." Page smoothed a hand over Dylan's back. "You just have to ask before you take. That's all."

Dylan nodded, his Adam's apple bobbing. "Thanks."

He grabbed the dish tub and hurried to the kitchen, his whole bearing lighter.

Page turned on me, voice colder than I'd ever heard it. "I told you to leave it alone."

"I didn't know. I thought he was hiding something."

"Exactly. And now you've embarrassed the boy."

I stood rooted. "You knew?"

"Of course I knew." Page's arms flew around her like a windmill. "I'm the one who told Kady to make sure there were leftovers for him to take home. His mom works two piddling jobs, and there's not always enough to feed all three kids."

I let out a slow breath. Another one of Page's strays. "I didn't mean to hurt him. I'm just trying to keep you from going to prison."

Page gave a nod, then headed back toward the checkout counter, thunder in her step. "Sometimes the secrets people keep aren't about guilt but survival."

NINE

Old Flames and New Lies

Four-thirty and night had already fallen all around me. At least the snow had stopped, so driving home wasn't too bad. I focused on the plowed ribbon of road. "I really messed up today, Harlan. I managed to shame a kid who was just trying to help out his family."

I imagined Harlan sitting on the passenger's side of the car, leaning an elbow on the door and shaking his head in small, slow arcs. "I told you to leave the investigation to the professionals."

"I can't. I can't let Page go to prison for a crime I know she didn't do. And Nolan's not doing anything to clear her. I'm trying to help my family—just like you."

"The difference is that I was an officer of the law, and you're not."

I turned into our neighborhood. That was when I saw the white Messer & Messer van with its tipped-over paint can logo in the Butlers' driveway. The real estate sign on top of the snowbank had a banner plastered across the bottom: Sold!

I understood the Butlers' desire to move into something smaller. They were getting on in years and wanted an easier living situation. It would be odd to have new neighbors after all these years, though. I hoped they were friendly.

I hesitated. By now Stella would be bursting to go out. I should go straight home. Before I'd fully thought about what I was doing, I'd turned into the driveway.

"This is a bad idea, Ellie," Harlan said.

"It's an opportunity." I shifted into Park. "I really need to talk to the boyfriend. You're the first to say that it's usually a partner."

"You're in the middle of nowhere. No one knows where you are. And you're going to talk to a possible murderer in an empty house. How is that not a recipe for disaster?"

"You worry too much."

"My job is to worry."

"Your supposed best friend isn't doing anything to help Page."

"If something goes wrong," Harlan said, "I can't help you."

"Everything's going to be fine." I turned off the engine and reached for my purse. I patted its side. "Besides, I have mace."

Purse hooked over my shoulder, I followed the winding path to the front door.

Music boomed from inside, so loudly my whole body thumped to its rhythm. Not a sad ballad or a quiet instrumental, but something harsh and angry, all bass and screaming vocals. My fist hovered over the door. Grief didn't sound like this, did it?

He wouldn't have heard a knock on the door, so I carefully opened the door and stepped inside. The smell of wet paint filled my lungs.

"Hello?" I called, but no one was going to hear anything over all that noise. I spotted a phone and a Bluetooth speaker on the floor of the living room on the left and, when the screen woke up, I hit the pause button.

"Hey!" someone shouted from the next room, then appeared, brandishing a paint roller covered with neutral beige paint like a weapon. "Who are you? What are you doing here?"

"I'm Ellie Hamlin. I'm Page's sister-in-law. From the bookshop. I was driving home and saw your van in the driveway, and I wanted to offer my condolences. For Kady's passing."

He lowered the paint roller to his side, dripping paint onto the drop cloth. His throat worked, and he gave one stiff nod. "Thanks."

"Have the police given you anything about who might have killed her?"

He made a sour face. "I think they think I did it."

"Why?"

He sneered. "Because I'm—I was—the boyfriend."

"Did you?"

A storm filled his eyes. "Of course not! I loved her. We were going to get married."

"I heard that you two broke up."

He shook his head. "We just had a disagreement. We were working it out."

"But all your stuff's gone from her attic."

He frowned as if he hadn't expected that. "How do you know that?"

I shrugged one shoulder. "Kady's mom mentioned the breakup and your moving out."

"Kady's mom didn't want to face the fact her daughter loved me." Something that looked a lot like hatred narrowed his gaze. "I wasn't good enough. I embarrassed her."

"How?"

He pulled on the collar of his paint-splattered white overalls. "My collar's too blue."

"That doesn't sound like Gayle." It totally did.

He snorted. "Apparently, my table manners were—how did she put it—'*unrefined*,' when she took us out to the country club to celebrate Kady's new job managing the café."

"I'm so sorry."

He dropped down on the third stair of the staircase going up. "She won't even let me plan anything for Kady's funeral."

"That's not fair, considering you were getting married."

A dejected look crossed his face. "Kady, she didn't like big fusses, and her mother's going to make a big fuss, make it all about the good doctor and her loss."

I sat beside him on the stair. From this angle, I spotted a half-full garbage bag in the hallway. Big and black—exactly like the one I'd seen draped over Kady's body in the dumpster. A chill climbed up my spine. Maybe Harlan was right. Maybe coming here alone was stupid. But now that I was here, I couldn't stop, could I?

"Where were you on Thursday night?" I asked, trying to make it sound as if it were no big deal.

He stiffened. "You're awfully nosy."

"Just curious."

"It's none of your business, but I was on a date."

"A date?" That seemed an odd move for someone professing to have been in love. "I thought you were trying to work it out with Kady."

He leaned the roller handle against the wall and rubbed the base of his neck hard. "I was trying to make her jealous. Wanted to make her see what she was missing out on."

"You said you loved her. Wanted to marry her."

He dropped his hands between his knees. "I do. I did. But things got...complicated."

What did that even mean? "How?"

He shook his head. "Doesn't matter now."

I had a feeling it mattered a lot.

"Where did you go on this date?" This was information I could check out.

"Why?" His tone turned icy. "You taking notes for the cops?"

I paused long enough to meet his gaze. "Thursday... That was the night she—"

"I know what night it was!" His face reddened and he looked away.

The silence stretched. Not a comfortable pause but the brittle kind that crackled with unsaid things. Secrets. The heater kicked on, a whisper through the floor vents, and the atmosphere suddenly turned stifling.

"Your date, did she wear a red scarf by any chance?"

"Didn't notice." He reached for the roller again, but instead of going back to work, he held it in front of his chest like a shield.

"You should leave now." His voice was flat, the edges smoothed down like someone trying too hard to sound calm.

"I just want to understand. That's all." I rose from the stair. "Page is my family, and she's taking Kady's death hard. I need to know what happened."

"I don't know." His jaw steeled. "I didn't kill her."

"Then you shouldn't mind me asking questions."

"I do mind." He dropped the roller into the paint tray in the hall, splattering paint drips onto the freshly painted wall. "You come in here, poke around, act like you know everything—"

"I don't, that's why I'm asking questions. You said you loved her. And now you're saying you were with someone else the night she died."

He took a step toward me, stopped and raked both hands through his hair. "I made a mistake, okay? People make mistakes. Doesn't mean I killed her."

My heart knocked against my ribs. "And people who make mistakes sometimes try to cover them up."

His gaze locked on mine. For a moment, something flickered—grief? Guilt? Red-hot anger?

"You need to go." His tone left no room for disagreement.

And Harlan was right; I was in the middle of nowhere with a possible murderer. I should take the exit he'd given me.

Behind him, the garbage bag slouched like a shadow near the wall. I couldn't unsee this possible clue.

I gave a slow nod. "Take care of yourself, Erik."

He didn't answer, but his icy gaze followed me right out the door.

———

BACK IN THE CAR, I SAT WITH MY HANDS CURLED around the steering wheel for a moment while the engine idled. The warmth from the vents did nothing to settle my nerves. I glanced at the living room windows. No movement. But still my stomach fluttered with uncertainty. He'd said he'd loved her. Yet, he'd gone out with another woman on the night Kady had died. Something the police could surely follow up on. I needed to know her time of death. And what time Erik had left that date.

The date may have been an elaborate ruse to set up an alibi.

Before I changed my mind, I dialed Nolan's personal number. I didn't give him a chance to say hello. "Messer &

Messer uses the same kind of garbage bags you found on Kady."

"What were you doing anywhere close to Messer?"

I put the car in reverse and backed out of the driveway. "He's working in my neighborhood. I just happened to notice the garbage bags. And check to see if he was on a date on Thursday night, with whom and what time he left."

"Leave it alone, Ellie." His voice held a warning growl.

I snorted. "In your capable hands."

TEN

Pastry Wars

On Tuesday morning, after I got everything going at the café and Bailey showed up for her shift, I decided to take a trek down the road to the Brightside Bakery. I tried to sneak out while Page was busy, but she somehow still caught me in the act.

"Where are you going?" she asked hands on hips. Today, she wore a white tunic with leopard print red hearts and black leggings with red and white hearts. Her hair was twisted into a relatively tame red heart claw hair clip.

"Out for a bit."

"I'll come with." She reached behind the counter and grabbed a red coat and her purple backpack purse. Stella got up from her bed behind the counter and stretched.

"You have a business to run."

"*Pfft!* Janelle's here."

Giving in was easier than fighting. Stella wagged her tail as if she expected to come along. I pointed at her bed and said, "Stay!"

I swear the dog pouted before making a show of turning back to her bed like a prisoner being shown to a cell. "She'll be okay with Janelle?"

Page chuckled. "Stella knows how to run the place."

We strolled down together, boots sloshing in the melting snow on the sidewalk. Bright sun pinged off the watery surface, making me wish I'd brought sunglasses for the glare.

"What's the plan?" Page asked, keeping pace.

So focused was I on my goal that I hadn't realized I was charging up the sidewalk like a racehorse. "Finding out more about Kady."

The Brightside Bakery smelled of brown sugar and cinnamon and buttery goodness. The place hummed with conversation at all the filled tables and the hiss of the espresso machine behind the counter —even more impressive than the coffee contraption at Page's café. Soft love songs floated through the air, tugging at my heart. Harlan used to croon "When You Kiss Me" in his off-key baritone, twirling me around the living room before reeling me in for a kiss.

Page headed straight to the pastry counter, hands on

the glass as if she were a little kid. "Look at all the variety! Maybe I should add more choices."

"I think you have plenty for a small café. You're a bookseller, remember? Not a bakery."

"But look at those donuts!" Rows of donuts filled a whole shelf in the pastry case—everything from apple cider donuts to heart-shaped jelly donuts to coconut-covered chocolate cake donuts.

Dani stepped out of the back. "Hi, ladies! Coming to check out the competition?"

"Just admiring." Page pointed at Dani's famous apple cider donuts. "I'll have one of those."

Dani chuckled and got out tongs and a bag. "Can't blame you. They're addictive."

She looked at me. "Do you want anything?"

"Same, please."

Once she'd bagged the donuts, I handed her a ten. Page didn't wait and dipped into her bag right away, taking a big bite of donut, and moaning with pleasure.

"You graduated from Hopewell's baking program, right? Same class as Kady Chilton?"

As she rang up the sale, Dani's smile slipped. "Yeah. Awful what happened to her. Do you have any news?"

"No, we're still trying to figure out who might've wanted her gone." I took my change. "How did she get along with her classmates?"

Dani toggled her head from side to side. "Well enough. She wasn't unpopular, but..." Her lips pressed tight. "Let's just say some people were put off by her... confidence."

"Confidence?" Since when was confidence a bad trait?

Dani pursed her bottom lip. "That palate of hers was one mad skill. The girl could taste a dessert and re-create it like some kind of baking savant."

Page took another loud bite of donut. "Like a superpower?"

"Exactly." Dani leaned her forearms over the wooden counter and lowered her voice. "She once nailed every ingredient in Chef Langley's seven-layer torte. Right down to the quarter teaspoon of Biber chile."

"Never heard of it," Page said around a bite of donut.

"It's a Turkish chile that has notes of chocolate, raisins and smoke." Dani lifted her brow. "Of course, that's when things went sideways."

"How?"

"Chef Langley had announced that the best final exam cake would get a feature in *New Hampshire Magazine* to promote the baking program. Marissa had worked on her recipe for weeks."

"Marissa Marchetti of Cake My Day?" Marissa, who was known for her chocolate love cake. A recipe I'd seen replicated in Kady's recipe sketchbook.

Dani nodded. Outside, sirens screamed up Main Street.

"But Kady won." Gayle must have gloated over having her daughter featured so prominently. Something she could brag about when she more often than not had complaints about her daughter's choices.

"Chef Langley said she'd elevated it." Dani swept a hand through the air. "Added this...mysterious element that took it over the top."

"Let me guess. Marissa didn't take it well?"

"She accused Kady of stealing her recipe. Kady swore up and down she just tasted it once at our practice session before the final."

Page tapped the counter like a patron at a bar. "Hit me again."

Dani reached into the case, chuckling. "Don't say I didn't warn you."

I rummaged through my purse and pulled out a page I'd photocopied from Kady's recipe sketchbook. "Recognize this?"

Dani took the page and ran a finger down the list of ingredients. She frowned. "Where did you get this? That's *almost* like my apple cider donut recipe."

"Almost?"

"She missed something small, but look at this—mace." She tapped a finger on the page. "That's my thing. Most people use nutmeg." Dani folded the page and tucked it into the pocket of her apron. "Can't have Page's new baker making my famous donuts."

"No worries. Page isn't going to add donuts to her offerings." I raised an eyebrow at Page.

"Wellll," Page said, taking another bite of donut. "I might. But not yours." She made an X across her heart. "Swear."

"Had she reverse-engineered other people's recipes?" I asked.

Dani shrugged one shoulder. "It might have happened a couple of other times, too. I used to joke that she'd ruin all our businesses before we could even open them. That copycat palate of hers could've put an indie baker out of a job."

"Marissa?" I asked. "Think she's still holding a grudge?"

"I mean, her specialty cake business is booming. Cake My Day has a months-long waitlist. But..." Dani hesitated. "I did see her and Kady arguing at the indoor farmers' market a few weeks ago."

"What about?"

"No idea. But it wasn't a friendly catch-up, if you get my drift."

Page licked a smear of glaze off her thumb. "Marissa once threatened to take back her cake from a venue because the client wanted her to add sprinkles. Said they clashed with her brand aesthetic."

Whatever happened to the client is always right? "So she doesn't let things go."

Dani leaned forward. Voice low, she said, "Let's just say I'd never want to cross her on a bad day. But murder?" Her mouth flattened. "That seems extreme."

Page polished off her second donut. "That's what everyone keeps saying."

I lifted the bag with my untouched donut. "Thanks, Dani. Let us know if you remember anything else."

I turned to leave, then thought of one last question. "Does Marissa wear a red scarf by any chance?"

Dani's eyes went wide. "Why, yes, she does! At least she did at the farmers' market."

As we walked out, an ambulance sat by the town square, red light swirling, turning the snowbanks pink like blood.

Page tipped her chin toward the drama. "I wonder what's going on there."

"Looks like a traffic accident. That corner needs reengineering."

Page tugged on my sleeve and headed toward the square. "Let's take the long way back to the bookshop."

"Fine. I need to think anyway." Maybe Marissa had gotten over the whole cake thing. But maybe she hadn't.

Some people didn't just hold grudges but enshrined them in crystal display cases.

Page stopped so suddenly I bumped into her. "Ellie—look!"

"What?"

"Isn't that Erik Messer's van?"

The front end of a white van with the paint can logo on the side was wrapped around a light pole. Two EMTs rolled a gurney toward the back of the ambulance. Even with all the blood covering his face, there was no mistaking the patient: Erik Messer.

Page trotted over to the EMTs. "Is he okay?"

"He hit his head pretty badly," one of the EMTs said.

They slid him into the ambulance and slammed the door shut.

As the ambulance pulled away, I glanced toward the van's open door. In the cup holder, a Purple Page Café cup with its distinctive purple paisley print glinted in the sun.

I grabbed Page's arm. "Let's get out of here."

"Why?"

"Because once the police see that cup, it'll give them one more piece of circumstantial evidence against you—and you're already on their radar as prime suspect."

———

PAGE CHARGED INTO THE BOOKSTORE AND disappeared into the back room without even acknowledging Janelle at the checkout desk. Janelle sent a "What's-up?" look my way, but I ignored her, too. Stella roused from her bed, looked from Page to me, then decided it was safer to go back to her cushion.

I headed for the kitchen, my happy place. The one place where I could let emotions work themselves out with a whisk and a warm oven.

Bailey peered into the kitchen, eyes big and wide like an owl's. "Is Page okay? Are you?"

I slammed my purse onto the top of the step stool, with a satisfying thud. Let my coat, hat and gloves follow. "One of the coffee cups from the café was found at the scene of an accident."

Bailey took a shy step into the kitchen, toying with the edge of her apron with both hands. "Oh. But I mean, that's not so strange, right? Lots of people drink coffee and drive. I must have filled at least twenty to-go cup orders this morning alone."

"Maybe, but not all of them are Kady's ex-boyfriend."

"Oh, wow." She blinked. "Still don't see what a coffee cup has to do with the accident."

I yanked mixing bowls from the shelf with more force than necessary. "Page is the prime suspect for Kady's murder, and the cup could make them think she wanted to get rid of the boyfriend for some reason."

"Or that he just stopped here to get coffee."

"Did you serve him?"

She shook her head. "I had Janelle man the café while I went to the bathroom."

Bailey toed a slow arc in front of her, staring at the floor as if it somehow held answers. "Do they really think Page did it?"

"She didn't." I rummaged through the pan rack for a 9 x 13-inch pan, then took out a couple more just to hear the tinny clatter. "I just have to prove it. Somehow."

"Can I help you with something?" Bailey stepped forward and gripped the edge of the table. Her voice was casual, but her face pinched with distress. As if I were invading her territory. In a way, I was. I'd turned down the baker's job and Bailey had accepted, so technically, this was her kitchen.

But I needed to think. And Page needed brownies. Or blondies. Or some sort of bar that might take the edge off the weight of worry she was carrying.

"Sorry," I muttered. "I bake when I'm stressed."

Bailey eyed the army of equipment I'd lined up. "I guess you're really stressed, then."

I reached for cocoa and vanilla. "Do you know Marissa Marchetti?"

Bailey nibbled a thumbnail. "Of Cake My Day?"

I nodded as I scooped flour into a bowl, a little too fast. A cloud of white dust rose and settled over the table like fog.

"Not personally, but I've heard of her. She bakes amazing cakes." She gave a quick shrug. "She also has a reputation for being...intense."

"Do you think she could have killed Kady?"

Bailey's eyes widened and her fingertips touched her chest. "Me? I— I don't know. That's a really heavy thing to say about someone."

I stuffed a glass bowl filled with pats of butter into the microwave, then let the whirr of the machine fill the quiet.

Bailey picked at a hangnail. "I mean, given the right circumstances, I think anyone could."

I stilled, my fingers curled around the measuring cup of brown sugar. The silence stretched long enough the refrigerator's motor hummed through my bones. The bowl in front of me seemed too empty, the waiting too expectant. The microwave beeped, sounding like a warning. I dumped the sugar, then the melted butter into the bowl.

Bailey stepped back, color blooming in her cheeks. "Have you thought that maybe... Page could've done something without meaning to? Like, I don't know, got pushed too far? Janelle was telling me that Kady was always late. And that got to Page."

The question hung there, sharp and pointed. I whisked the butter and sugar—hard—until the mixture was smooth. I reached for the eggs, then cracked one on the tabletop, crumbling the shell into shards, spilling white and yolk into a mess.

"You don't know Page. She couldn't even if she tried." With a wad of paper towels, I swept the wet egg mess into the garbage can.

"Okay." She gave a tiny nod. "Let me know if you need anything."

I grabbed another egg. "She didn't do it," I said again —more to myself than to her.

ELEVEN

Copycat Cupcake

By the time I'd calmed down enough to stop baking and head home, my car wouldn't start. Stella sat in the back seat, staring at me as if asking why we weren't moving. I called Jim at the garage. He took a quick look under the hood and declared I needed a new battery. "I gotta order the part, so it'll be morning before you're set."

"Thanks."

Jim hooked my car to the tow truck and beeped his horn as he left.

I trudged back inside the bookshop, Stella in tow. "Looks like I'm stuck here unless you can give me a ride home."

Page nibbled on a brownie while closing out the cash

register. "I was going to ask if I could come over to your place tonight."

"Bert out of town?"

She nodded. "I was thinking that we could stop at Marissa's cottage on the way."

"Kind of late, don't you think?" Only six, but in February, the nights were long and today seemed to have gone on forever. And driving in the dark wasn't my favorite thing.

"Then she won't be expecting us." Page stuffed the register's take into the safe. "Which makes it perfect."

Bailey left with a wave and a goodbye. I helped Page close up, then we headed toward Brighton Lake. Marissa's "cottage" was right off Lakeshore Drive in a posh development on the northeast side of the lake. Her cottage was less Hansel and Gretel and more French Provençal—golden stone, tall windows, gray slate roof she probably had to get raked weekly.

She answered the door with brows and lips puckered in a sour lemon way. Her dark hair was pulled back into a tight bun and held in place by a beige headband. "Did we have an appointment?"

I glued on a smile. "We'd just like a quick word."

Though she barely reached my chin, her demeanor made her seem twice as tall. She eyed us up and down. "It's not convenient right now. I'm in the middle of assembling a five-tier cake."

"This won't take long."

"I don't do drop-ins." Her gaze dropped to Stella. "That thing can't come in. This is a working kitchen."

"She's clean, quiet and obedient."

"It's against the health code." She didn't budge.

Page stepped in, voice sugarcoated. "It's about Kady."

Marissa's jaw tensed. She glanced behind her, then let the door open another few inches. "Fine. But that dog stays *right there* on the mat."

Stella whined. I patted her head and murmured, "Stay."

Her gaze flickered between me and Marissa, but she sank obediently to her haunches on the mat.

Inside, I noticed the scarf right away—red cashmere, and as June had said, long enough to lasso a cow. It lay draped over a peg above Marissa's sleek camel reefer coat. I caught Page's gaze and gave a small nod toward it. Her eyes widened.

Marissa caught the look. "Something wrong with my coat?"

"Just admiring the color," I said.

She led us through a narrow hallway into a glowing kitchen painted a buttery gold with white cabinets and a terracotta floor. Ovens pumped out warmth. On a large country table stood two tiers of white cake stacked on top of each other. Three more waited on cooling racks. The air smelled heavenly—sugar, lime, and something piney.

"What smells so good?" I asked.

"Gin and tonic cake for a party tomorrow, and I still have a lot of work to do. So, let's skip the idle chatter, shall we?" She stabbed three dowels into a cake layer as if she were settling a score. "You want to know about Kady."

"You had an argument with her at the café last week," I said. "From what I heard, it got pretty heated. One that made you angry enough to kill her?"

She flipped away my comment with the back of one hand. "Please! She wasn't worth it."

"But you were angry enough to confront her."

She sent me a cutting look. "Wouldn't you if someone stole something of yours? I was just putting her on notice that I wasn't going to stand for her copycat theft any longer."

"Did she try to copy one of your recipes?"

"Not tried. Did. My chocolate love cake in school. And just last month, my dark chocolate coconut passion fruit mousse cake." She paused to lower another tier of cake onto the dowels with exacting care. "She had the nerve to turn my elegant cake into cupcakes. Cupcakes!" She snorted. "As if!"

"You can't copyright recipe ingredients," Page said, dabbing a finger into stray cake crumbs.

Marissa spun on her, pointing a red-manicured finger like a dagger. "Do you have any idea how long it takes to perfect a recipe?"

We both shook our heads. I baked from other people's recipes I got online or from a cookbook. Page didn't bake at all.

"It takes a *long* time. Weeks. Months. Trial and error. Subtle adjustments. And that...that *magpie* thought she could just snatch my hard work!" Marissa put down the layer she was just about to stack onto the dowels. Hands planted on the table, she reset her rising temper with a long breath. "She thought she was so clever. Reverse-engineering recipes. And she did—right down to the coconut rum." Marissa made a snapping motion with her fingers. "Not one original thought in that girl's head. That's why she had to steal."

"How did you find out about the copycat cupcakes?"

She focused on placing the next layer just so. "A friend happened to buy one from the café and thought it tasted remarkably like my cake."

"You confronted Kady about it?"

"At the farmers' market a couple of weeks ago. She denied everything. Said she'd never made the recipe. So, I brought a piece of her own cupcake to the café and asked her again."

The Golden Girls had missed that part of the exchange. "And?"

"She lied. Right to my face. I told her to cut the garbage, or I'd go public."

Page reached for more cake crumbs. "Yikes. I had no idea."

"Well, you should vet your bakers better."

"Kady's dead," I said. "So your troubles are over."

Marissa examined the cake from all angles, adjusting it with surgeon-like precision. "I wanted her to stop stealing. Not die."

Marissa placed the last layer onto the dowels. A satisfied look crossed her face.

She crossed her arms under her chest and leaned her rear against the table. "Look, you own your own business. You know what it's like. You have to protect your interests. And Kady was infringing on mine. I simply asked her to cease and desist. Then I left. I haven't seen her since."

"Any chance you'd give us a copy of your recipe so we could compare it to Kady's bake book?" I asked.

Marissa gave a sharp, humorless laugh. "I'm not handing you my intellectual property on a silver platter."

"That's fair," I said. "What if we read the ingredients to you?"

Marissa sighed. "Fine. I'll let you know if the ingredients match up." She lifted a finger. "One condition."

"What?"

"If she does have that recipe, you burn it."

Page stuck out her hand. "Deal."

———

WE DROVE BACK TO THE BOOKSHOP AND HEADED straight for the bakery book, Stella trotting in after us. Page thumbed through the pages, then stopped.

"There it is," she said, turning the book for me to see. "Dark chocolate coconut passionfruit mousse cupcakes."

Something looked off about the page. The type and layout were the same—black ink on white copy paper. Times font. But the print was lighter. Fainter. Not like the others. I flipped through the book and spotted a handful of other recipes with the same barely there ink. Copies of copies, maybe? Or printed on a different printer?

I dialed Marissa's number.

She picked up on the first ring.

"I've got the recipe in front of me," I said. "Are you ready?"

"Go."

"One hundred fifty milliliters of vegetable oil, 200

grams of flour, 280 grams of light brown sugar…" I went down the whole two-page list of ingredients.

"She got every single ingredient." Her voice rang with disbelief.

"You're sure."

"A recipe that complete didn't walk into someone's brain." Marissa's tone was frosty. "I don't care how good her palate was. She *stole* my recipe. Had to."

"I'll make sure it's gone from the bake book." I pulled the sheet from the plastic protector and got ready to burn it.

After a beat of silence, Marissa said, "I didn't kill her, but if she was alive, we'd go another round."

TWELVE

Tangled Truths

"When was the last time you had a haircut?" I asked Page the next morning after I'd finished my set-up at the café. I'd woken up with an idea on how to have a chat with Samantha Garvey, with whom Kady had apparently still been friends. Samantha just happened to own Sam's Signature Salon up a little way on Main Street.

Page, busy going through some paperwork at the checkout desk, glanced at me over the top of her reading glasses, suspicious. "I don't know. A while. Why?"

"It shows." I reached for her coat, a black one today, draped over her rolling chair. "My treat."

She shook the paper in her hand. "Kinda busy right now."

"I took the first available appointment." I glanced at

my watch. "Starts in ten minutes. Come on. Two for one. New look for you." I leaned closer. "Maybe a new lead for us."

Her gaze narrowed. "You're using me as bait."

"I prefer the term 'creative strategy.'"

Page rolled her eyes, but the amateur sleuth in her was piqued. "Janelle!" she called out. "I'm going out for a bit. Bailey will be here soon."

"Okay," came a muffled voice from the back room.

"I need you out here."

Janelle peeked out, eyes wide behind her owlish glasses. "Okay."

I tugged Page's sleeve. "Come on, or we'll be late. Sam runs that salon like a drill sergeant." The mean girl in her hadn't quite disappeared. "Tardiness could cut our chance of talking with her."

Chased by the winter chill and the scud of heavy clouds in the sky, we racewalked up Main Street and arrived a little winded. Sam's Signature Salon welcomed us with warm air scented with jasmine and sandalwood. Soft spa music floated from unseen speakers. Shabby chic mirrors, soft peach walls, and a vintage cart full of products with French names I couldn't pronounce gave the place an air of a curated Instagram feed. Definitely not Page's style.

Samantha stood behind a styling chair, uncoiling a flat

iron cord and plugging it into an outlet. Her ash-blonde bob was so sharply angled it looked almost architectural.

She turned and slanted Page an evil genius smile. "Page! You're finally ready to let me fix that...situation?" She waved a manicured hand at Page's frizzy hair, which had become a dry mess with all the artificial heat.

Page shot me a glare before smoothing a hand over her messy curls. "You owe me for this."

I laughed. "You'll thank me when Sam's worked her magic."

Sam ushered Page into a chair with the air of a surgeon prepping for a delicate operation. "Ellie's right. You'll be a new woman after I'm done."

Sam soon had Page shampooed and sipping rosehip tea from a dainty teacup. She sectioned Page's hair and combed it with a quick, practiced hand. I perched on a nearby chair, pretending interest in the stack of surprisingly current gossip magazines until the air filled with the regular *snip-snip* of scissors.

"Any news on Kady?" Sam asked, staring at the back of Page's head like a sculptor stared at marble.

"No." Page shook her head. "I can't believe she's gone."

I closed the magazine on my lap. "You were friends with her, right? I remembered you, Ashley and Kady being thick as thieves in middle school." Mostly I remember Sam and Ashley getting Kady in trouble, but best to avoid that tidbit.

"We kept in touch." Sam turned Page away from the mirror and continued trimming. "Tried to, anyway. Everyone's busy. Work. Life. You know how it is."

"Seems to get tougher the older you get." Life had a way of cutting ties. "When did you last see her?"

"She came in about two weeks ago."

Page's hands popped out from under the gold cape. "Did she seem worried about anything?"

Sam's mouth flattened into a straight line, and she snipped faster.

"Did she ever talk about Erik?" I chimed in.

That got me a twitch of cheek. "They were... complicated."

I exaggerated a frown. "Did he treat her badly?"

"No, no," Sam focused on Page's hair, testing the length on each side to make sure the cut was even. "Nothing like that."

"Then what?" I asked.

Sam avoided both our gazes and ran her fingers through Page's shorter do. "I don't gossip about my clients."

"You were friends too," I said. "And friends talk."

"Doesn't mean I break confidence." Sam sighed and armed herself with a blow dryer and a round brush.

"We're not asking for idle gossip," Page said. "We're asking because she's dead. And I'm the one everyone's looking at like I killed her just because she worked for me."

Sam hesitated.

"Help us find who really did hurt her," Page whispered.

Sam sighed, long and low. The blow dryer whirred to life. Conversation died under the roar. Page gave me a helpless look in the mirror. I gave a one-shoulder shrug.

When the dryer cut off, Sam paused, hand still wrapped tightly around the handle. "Kady canceled her last appointment."

Page met my gaze in the mirror.

"Did something happen?" I asked.

Sam slowly set the dryer into its holster by the side of the mirror. Her reflection in the mirror looked older, weighed down. She picked up a comb and tugged through Page's hair a little too roughly, making Page wince. "If my clients get wind of me breaking confidence, then I lose their trust. The stylist-client relationship is sacred, you know."

"It's not breaking trust if it helps us figure out who killed her," I said, trying to keep the exasperation out of my voice. "It's doing right by your friend."

Sam puffed out a breath. "I suppose it's going to come out in the autopsy anyway."

I waited, not pushing. A trick I'd seen Harlan use many times when the kids were younger, and it always had them blurting out something they didn't want to admit.

Forehead pleated, Sam attacked Page's hair with a flat iron with slow, precise strokes. "She said she was tired. She canceled her color, saying it was toxic. Switched to herbal tea from her regular coffee." She swallowed hard. "Said she had something on her mind."

The pieces clicked in place. I gasped. "Kady was pregnant."

That changed everything—and pointed the finger back in Erik's direction.

Sam nodded. "She'd just found out. Was still getting used to the idea."

I tried to keep my voice steady. "Was she happy about it?"

Sam gave a watery smile. "Yeah. She was. Nervous, you know, but...happy. Like this was the start of something good."

"And Erik?" I asked. "What did he think?"

"She said she was waiting for the right time. That he needed to hear it the right way. Whatever that means."

"But he didn't know?" I pressed.

The flat iron got too close to Page's ear, and she yelped.

"Sorry." Sam continued ironing Page's curls. "I don't

know. She just said she was planning on telling him soon." Her voice dropped. "She was...hopeful."

Hopeful didn't sound good.

The knotted ball in my stomach grew tighter.

Sam smoothed Page's hair with a brush, then picked up a mirror and showed her the back.

Page stared at herself in the mirror, her newly layered hair soft and glossy around her shoulders. "You're right, Sam. This looks great!"

Sam pulled two bottles from the cart. "Moisturizing shampoo and conditioner. Use them both. Don't let the frizz win."

Page grinned and handed me the bottles. "Your treat, right?"

I looked at the sticker and gulped. "Totally worth it."

As we stepped out into the icy wind again, Page zipped her coat halfway. "Are you thinking what I'm thinking?"

"If Erik didn't know, we need to tell him."

"And if he did know?"

I looked out across Main Street, where the clouds had thickened to iron. "We need to know how he reacted to the news."

THIRTEEN

One Step Forward, Two Steps Back

I dropped Page off at the bookshop, leaving Stella there, then headed to the hospital in Hopewell. The tires swished on the wet roads, but I barely noticed. My thoughts were stuck in a loop, whooshing in time to the windshield wipers—Kady's murder, her pregnancy, the half-truths and evasions at every turn. Page's name on the tip of everyone's tongue like a loaded indictment.

I had to get there before Erik was released. I might not get another chance to confront him. And I needed answers. And the one good thing about gossip was that I knew the ambulance had taken him to Hopewell Community Hospital, which meant his injuries weren't life threatening.

At the hospital, I stopped by the gift store and picked up the saddest bouquet of carnations—white and wilted, their edges browning. Perfect. Just enough to make my visit seem polite, not personal.

I took the elevator to the third floor, heart thudding. The hallways smelled of sanitizer and sadness. And my own sorrow was close to the surface here. The last place I'd seen Harlan, touched him. The doctors had tried to revive him and left him bruised, battered and bloodied. The goodbye in that small room so impossible even though I knew he was no longer in his body.

I shook my head and took in a breath. *Focus on the now.*

I didn't know what I expected, but I told myself I was ready for anything. I kept my stride steady, scanning the paper nameplates on the doors. Erik's name appeared on the next-to-last room's. A quiet corner, thankfully away from the nurses' station.

I knocked and walked in without waiting. "Hi."

He was propped up in bed, skin pale, dark circles under his eyes. A bandage circled his head, and a sling supported his right arm. The second he saw me, his expression turned to stone.

"You!" He tried to sit up straighter and winced. "What are you doing here?"

"I came to see how you were doing after your accident." I held out the carnations. "It's what people do when they know someone is in the hospital."

He eyed the bouquet as if it hid explosives. "Don't insult my intelligence. You're here to dig again."

I set the bouquet on the rolling table beside the bed. "I'm here because I want to find who really killed Kady. That's it."

"You think I did it." He crossed his arms—or tried to —but the sling made the action awkward.

"I think everyone has secrets. Including you."

He snorted and turned his face toward the window. "Someone tried to kill me."

"What makes you say that?"

He glanced back at me, mouth set in a grim line. "There's no other explanation. The coffee—I didn't feel right. My vision blurred. Everything went black. One minute I was driving, the next the front of the van was wrapped around a lamppost. I could've died."

"Maybe you were distracted." I sank into one of the chairs by the bed. "Texting. Fiddling with the radio. Thinking about your last argument with Kady."

"I don't text and drive!"

I held his gaze. "You could've drugged the coffee your-self to get people talking. Stir up suspicion around Page. Then planted the cup with her logo right there in the cupholder—to make sure it got noticed." I turned my phone in his direction, showing him a snapshot of the

Purple Page cup in his van's cupholder. "That's bold. And stupid. You could've hurt someone else too."

His gaze narrowed. "That's twisted, even for you."

I shrugged. "So is murder."

"I didn't drug myself. I didn't murder Kady."

"Why get the coffee at the café then? There are two other places on Main Street that offer to-go coffee."

He blinked. "It's where I always went. Habit."

"Kady's dead. She doesn't work there anymore."

He hesitated, toying with the edge of the sheet. "Didn't matter."

A pause stretched between us. I leaned in. "Did you know Kady was pregnant?"

His jaw tightened. He didn't answer right away. Then his shoulders sank, and he nodded. The movement was slow, miserable. As if he were confessing something shameful.

"And?"

He glanced up. "What?"

"How did you feel about becoming a father?"

He picked at the tape holding the IV needle in place. "I may not have reacted in the best way."

"You bashed her in the head with a rolling pin?"

He recoiled. "What? No!" A flash of pain crossed his face. "I asked her to...you know..."

"No, I don't."

His voice turned small. "Get rid of it."

There it was, the irritation, the fear, the immaturity. "And when she refused?"

"I left." He folded and refolded the edge of the sheet covering him. "Cleaned out my stuff from her place and moved into my dad's basement." He lifted his unslinged arm in a helpless gesture, dragging the IV line with him. "I wasn't ready. I—" He shook his head, gaze falling into his lap. "I didn't want to raise a kid on scraps."

"Kady had money," I reminded him. "She had a hefty trust fund coming due in April. Money was never going to be a problem."

"My kid," he said between gritted teeth. "My responsibility."

His voice cracked at the edges. For a second, I saw past the stubborn defensiveness to the fear and the shame. The not-good-enough for the mighty Chiltons.

I didn't let up. I couldn't with Page's freedom on the line. "So, Thursday night, after your date, you went to see Kady..."

He shook his head. "I haven't seen her since she told me, you know, about the baby."

"Except for the coffee runs."

He nodded once. "She didn't talk to me."

"You still came."

"I kept hoping..."

"Where were you Thursday night, after your date?"

"My dad's place. He found the painting I was working on. Lost his mind. Said I was wasting my future. That I should be grateful he was handing me his company. That *that* was a solid future. Not airy-fairy stuff." He barked a laugh. "As if I asked for his hand-me-downs."

"I'm sure that didn't last all night."

"Sure felt like it." He washed a hand over his face, lost, it seemed, in a memory. "Cranked the music and painted until my hand hurt."

He reached for his phone, awkward with the IV line tugging at him. After some scrolling, he held it up to show me a photo.

The painting was...stunning. A love note, an apology, an expression of hope—him, Kady and the baby bathed in golden warmth.

"I love her." His voice broke and tears slid down his cheeks.

I stared at the screen. I understood grief. The weight of it. The guilt of it. The loneliness of it. If he was acting, he deserved an Oscar. But something in my gut held me back from writing him off as innocent just yet. I couldn't let my own grief inform what he exhibited. I was so tired of being wrong. So tired of second-guessing myself. Everything I unearthed seemed to make Page look more guilty—the opposite of my goal.

Maybe Harlan was right. Maybe I should let the professionals do their jobs. They couldn't do any worse than I was.

Before I could say anything more, the door cracked open, and a nurse poked her head in. "Sorry, ma'am. Visiting hours are up for now. You can come back later this afternoon."

I stood slowly, my mind spinning. "Thanks for your time."

Erik didn't answer. He turned away from me to stare out the window. Then softly, almost like an afterthought, he said, "She always said I had the power to break her heart. Guess she was right."

I left the room with more questions than I'd arrived with. I didn't know whether I'd just spoken with a grieving man or a master manipulator.

Either way, I hadn't found what I'd come for.

I was back to square one.

———

"WHAT ARE YOU DOING HERE?" NOLAN ASKED, AS I stepped out of Erik's hospital room. His voice was clipped, his gaze slicing.

I shifted my bag forward. "Visiting."

"I told you to stay out of this." His jaw ticked as if part

of him were holding back. He looked as if he hadn't slept in a while—eyes bloodshot, skin pale beneath a scruff of beard, hair unkempt.

"I just wanted to make sure he was okay."

Nolan lifted an arm and motioned me forward. "Walk with me."

He didn't wait. I fell into step, our boots echoing on the beige linoleum. In silence, we descended two flights of stairs and stepped into the lobby. There, floor-to-ceiling windows framed a bleak gray sky, drab buildings and a sleet-slicked road. The smell of rich coffee and toasted bagels from the coffee shop reminded me I hadn't eaten all day.

Nolan paced in front of the windows like a caged panther. I lowered myself into one of the armchairs, though every part of me wanted to pace, too.

"Anything new in the investigation?" I kept my voice careful, neutral.

"You know I can't discuss—"

"But you will."

He stopped, turned, then crouched so that we were eye to eye. His face looked older, lines cut deeper, eyes dull—as if the weight of the job were taking its toll. "It's not looking good for Page."

A chill ran down my spine. "What do you mean?"

"The coffee Messer got from her café was drugged with sleeping pills."

"What?" I tried to stand, but Nolan's big body blocked my way.

"Messer kept insisting someone had tried to kill him, so I had the coffee tested."

"It wasn't Page! She wasn't even *there* that morning."

He stood. "We're looking into it."

"Not hard enough!" I jumped up from the armchair. "Page didn't do this. She had no reason—"

He cut in. "We'll bring him in for questioning after he's released tomorrow."

My gut buzzed in alarm. "Something new come up?"

He pinched his nape with a hand.

"Nolan."

"Just let me handle it, okay?"

"You know I can't. Page's entire life is on the line."

He exhaled sharply, turning as if to walk away, then swung back. "The autopsy report came back."

"Oh." Everything in me stilled. "And? How did she die?"

"Strangulation."

I nodded, jaw tight. Strangulation was close, angry... personal. "Page isn't strong enough. Kady was younger. Stronger. Page isn't violent—"

He tilted his head. "You know better than that."

"Kady was pregnant," I blurted out. "You need to look at Erik more closely."

"How do you know that?"

I gave a small one-shoulder shrug. "People tell me things."

He stuffed his hands in the pockets of his gray topcoat. "Erik's alibis hold up."

"I know. He was at Bob's House until closing on Thursday. Doesn't mean he didn't go to Kady's after."

"Problem is," Nolan said, "she didn't die on Thursday."

The bottom dropped out of my stomach. "What do you mean? Thursday night is the last time Page saw Kady alive."

"According to the medical examiner, time of death was sometime between late Friday night and early Saturday morning. The cold makes it hard to pin down the exact time."

His words hit me like a punch to the chest. Friday night into Saturday morning. Page had opened the café on Saturday morning. Alone. That put her right back in the number one suspect spot. "Does Erik have an alibi for that time span?"

Nolan gave one sharp nod.

So that was it. Page was back in the crosshairs, and Erik was free and clear.

"This doesn't make sense." My mind spun, scrambling for something to hold on to. "Page had no reason to kill Kady, or try to hurt Erik. She has no motive, Nolan."

I hated the look on his face—as if he believed Page could've done it. As if he were already giving up.

I brushed past him, heart pounding. Hand ready to push open the hospital doors, I speared him with a glare. "I'm going to prove you're wrong."

FOURTEEN

Rewind

The force of my intentions died on the way back to the bookshop. I needed food, then I needed to lay out everything we had and see where I'd gone wrong. I had to have missed something. Because the one thing I knew was that Page hadn't killed Kady. Which meant that someone else had and wanted Page to take the fall.

Everything was just too well orchestrated.

I checked in on Stella, who turned her back on me as if miffed at my lack of attention all day. I made myself a turkey BLT sandwich and a cup of coffee in the café's kitchen, then took up residence at the far table along the wall, where I hoped no one would bother me.

In the lull between lunch and the after-school uptick, Page joined me. Stella settled at her feet.

"What are you doing?"

I'd written down every piece of information I had about Kady's murder on index cards and arranged them like a giant sliding puzzle on the tabletop. But nothing laid out smoothly. Even the timeline wavered, depending on whom I talked to. And no matter how many times I tried to complete the picture with something different, the final image kept snapping back to Page.

Some of the pieces didn't fit at all. Like Nate. I kept seeing him at the back door on Monday, shoulders tense, one hand shoved deep in his pocket as if protecting something. He'd left in a hurry, as if he couldn't wait to get away. What didn't he want us to see?

"Trying to figure out where I took a wrong turn." I looked up from my various notes. "And keep you out of prison."

"That would be nice because I absolutely didn't kill my baker." Her hair still looked smooth and sleek from this morning's styling at Sam's salon, giving her an air of vulnerability I hadn't seen since she was eighteen and left our home after an argument with Harlan.

"Someone is working really hard to make sure the police think so," I said. "Nolan said she died sometime between late Friday night and early Saturday morning."

"But I didn't see her on Friday. Or Saturday. Doesn't that prove I couldn't have killed her?"

"Except that you opened alone on Saturday morning. You spent an hour alone at the bookshop before leaving again to come to my place."

"But I didn't know she was already dead."

"Whoever did this had to be strong enough to lift her into the dumpster. They had to have the time and privacy to stage her body the way they did, so I'm guessing the actual time was closer to Friday night than early Saturday. Or you would've caught them in the act."

Page tutted. "I should've had that camera fixed a long time ago."

Of course she should have, but pointing out the obvious was only going to make her feel worse. "What about inside the store?"

"The whole system was connected." Page got out her phone and sent out a text, then gave me a quick smile. "Better late than never."

"So, whoever killed Kady knew the cameras weren't working. Someone that's here often enough to notice."

She flicked a hand at my index card puzzle. "That's literally our whole suspect list."

I looked at the cards—suspects, alibis, motives—spread across the table. This reminded me of the kind of puzzle where all the pieces were the same color and a handful of pieces were missing—impossible to finish.

Page plucked Dylan's card. "I know he had a crush on Kady, but he didn't kill her."

"You're probably right." His focus was on helping to feed his sisters, not on dating.

Page turned the card upside down, away from the grid. "Take Dave and Janelle off too."

A love of freshly baked brownies didn't seem like a viable reason for killing Kady. And Janelle could barely lift a dictionary, let alone a body. I put them aside but not away. "We might need to revisit them later."

Bailey approached, carrying two mugs of the Fall in Love tea—the February special—with notes of apple, cinnamon and vanilla. "Thought you could use a refill."

She set the steaming mugs on the table. "That looks like a puzzle."

Page tsked. "The Page-killed-Kady puzzle."

"Can I help?" She pulled out a chair and sat.

I drank in the warm aroma of the tea, hoping it would stir my brain cells into seeing the missing piece. "You don't really know any of the players."

"Sometimes a fresh look helps." She leaned her forearms on the table and studied the grid.

"I'm missing something." I got up and stretched. That's when I remembered the photos I'd taken in Harlan's—Nolan's—office. "I need to use your printer."

"Okay," Page said, gaze still on the grid, hand absently petting Stella's ears.

I headed toward the back room where the sound of whirring came through the closed door. As soon as I opened the door, the noise stopped and Janelle looked up, owlish eyes blinking as if she'd been caught in the act.

"What are you doing?" I asked.

"Shredding." She fed another handful of pages into the shredder, reviving the whirring noise.

That girl was so irritating. It took all I had not to shake her. "What are you shredding?"

"I dunno. Whatever Page said she needed gone."

That absolutely did *not* sound good. For a second, I wondered whether Page had something to hide, then chastised myself for even thinking the thought. I plucked a file folder from the pile. Business record. Why was Page shredding business records?

I headed toward the computer, sent the photos of Kady's file from my phone to my email, then printed them. That way, I'd have a cloud copy as well as a hard copy.

Back at the table, I laid out the photos alongside our suspects and list of evidence. The evidence against Page looked even worse in black and white. "Someone really wants to hurt you, Page."

Bailey frowned. "But why?"

"If we knew that, we wouldn't be in this situation."

"I can't think of anyone who has a reason to hate me this much."

Neither could I.

Bailey pointed at the rolling pin, bagged paper pieces, glasses, keys and apron. "Who had access to all this stuff?"

"Not Dave." Page moved him from the maybe pile to the no pile. "I don't think he's ever stayed long enough to go into the café. Always worried about his schedule."

Page reached for another card. "Dylan always rushes home to take care of his little sisters before his mom leaves for her night job."

That was rough for a young kid. He should've been enjoying his teenage years, playing sports, going out with friends, not working an after-school job and taking care of his younger siblings.

"Same with Janelle." Page added Janelle's card to the pile. "Now that Diana's MS is getting worse, she's the nighttime carer. She couldn't risk leaving her mom alone long enough to murder and cover up."

"Speaking of Janelle," I said, attempting to warm my cold hands around the mug of tea. "I saw her shredding papers in your office."

"Apparently, you don't need to keep records in perpetuity." Page tutted. "I needed space in the filing cabinets, so I'm having Janelle shred old records."

I looked at the three suspect cards left. "That leaves Erik, Nate and Marissa." I flicked a finger against Erik's. "And I don't think Erik did it."

"Why not?" Bailey asked. "Isn't it usually the boyfriend?"

I shook my head. "According to Nolan, he has a solid alibi for the time of death."

Bailey glanced at Marissa's card. "Didn't you say she and Kady had a fight a week before she died?"

Page nodded. "Kady reverse-engineered one of her recipes. Marissa was sure Kady had stolen it."

"That could make someone pretty angry," Bailey said. "And that type of anger sticks."

"Maybe," Page said. "But still... as hotheaded as she is, she doesn't strike me as the murdering type."

"And what does the murdering type look like?"

Bailey had a point.

I tapped the photo of the chocolate-covered espresso beans spilling out of Kady's mouth. "Where did you get those?"

Page leaned closer. "I don't know. Kady made some sort of muffin and decorated them with those. But that was weeks ago. As long as she kept to her budget, I didn't micromanage her spending."

I picked up the photo and stared at those beans as if they held an answer, if only I could look at them the right way. "Nate said they didn't come from him, but he was acting as if he was hiding something."

"Or maybe he didn't like being cornered." Bailey folded a paper napkin into smaller and smaller triangles. "People get jumpy when they're put on the spot."

That was true, but the image of him walking away—shoulders tight, hand buried in his pocket as if protecting something—wouldn't leave me.

Page sighed. "We're just going in circles."

Bailey gave her an encouraging smile. "But you're narrowing down. You went from six suspects down to two. That's something, right?"

"You're right." I stacked the cards into a neat pile. "We need to talk to Nate and Marissa again."

I added the photos to the pile and stuffed everything in my purse. Then I took out my phone and looked up the website for Stoneley Coffee Roastery Company. They had two sites: a storefront in Stoneley Village and the roastery on the outskirts of town.

I reached for my coat. "We'll probably find Nate at the roastery. Let's go."

"If he didn't do it, then maybe he saw something." Page headed toward the checkout counter for her coat.

Bailey picked up the empty mugs, fingers tight around the handles. "Just be careful, okay? I like this job and want to keep it. Whoever did this...they've already killed once."

"We're just asking questions." I hooked the purse strap over my shoulder. Stella danced around my feet at the prospect of going out.

Bailey frowned more deeply. "That's when people can get dangerous."

ONCE AT THE STONELEY COFFEE ROASTERY, I parked and left Stella in the car, snuggled in her fluffy blanket. She whined to join us, but I wasn't sure what kind of machinery we'd find there and I wanted to keep her safe. "I'll be right back."

The wintry wind hustled Page and me through the half-lifted bay door of the warehouse. Like icy fingers, the cold picked at every inch of exposed skin. Inside, the air was warmer and heavy with the earthy perfume of roasted coffee beans and the hum of machinery.

The warehouse stretched deep, lit by overhead LED bay fixtures. Burlap bags leaned in shadowed rows, their faded stencils whispering of far-away places—Sumatra, Guatemala, Ethiopia. Somewhere in the back a grinder let out a steady growl, releasing bursts of espresso so rich it coated my tongue.

At a long workbench, Nate slid brown five-pound bags

of beans into a shipping box, sealing it with a brisk *rrrip* of packing tape.

"Not a good time," Nate said, without looking up. His black beanie cast a shadow over his eyes, and his movements were as clipped as his tone. "My helper didn't show up, and I've got to get this order filled before tomorrow."

My boots scuffed against scattered beans on the concrete floor. "We won't keep you long."

"Like last time." He scoffed, pressing the tape down with extra force.

"We're here about Kady," Page said, voice soft and kind.

That earned her a glance—quick and wary—before Nate looked away again. "Talk to the cops. I've told them everything I know."

"Did you tell them why Kady was crying the last time you saw her?" I asked.

His jaw worked.

I pressed. "Kady trusted you with something."

The tape gun stilled for the briefest second before moving again. "I have no idea where you got that notion."

From the way you were holding your pocket on Monday. "Whatever it was, she's no longer here. Which means someone else, someone who already got away with killing her, could come after you if they find out you have it."

That landed. He dropped the tape gun on the bench

and gave me a sharp look. "You're twisting this. You don't know anything."

"What I do know is that she wouldn't want you to end up like her because you kept quiet."

Nate moved the sealed box from the bench to a dolly beside him.

The grinder's hum filled the silence, then the machine sputtered to a stop. Outside, the wind rattled the bay door, a steady reminder of the cold outside.

Nate looked toward the back office, then at me. "I feel like I'm betraying her confidence."

"If it means stopping a murderer before they kill again, then it's not betrayal."

His gaze speared Page's as if he wanted her to back him up. But Page, being the prime suspect, had even more riding on his answer than me. His gaze hardened. His jaw twitched.

For a moment, it seemed as if he would kick us out and keep Kady's secret locked away. Then he exhaled and said, "Wait here."

He vanished into the office. A chair scraped. A drawer slid. Paper slipped against paper. Then nothing.

My pulse drummed in my ears. Had he escaped out the back, taking Kady's secret with him?

Then Nate reappeared, face blank, carrying a plain white envelope folded in half—just the right size to fit in a pocket. He held it as if it contained anthrax. He stopped a foot away and searched my gaze.

"She wanted me to hold this for her. I don't know what's inside." His voice was low. "Or what I was supposed to do with it. Only that she was scared. Once you open it, you could find more than you bargained for."

A risk I was willing to take. I reached for the envelope, throat suddenly dry. I opened it just enough to read the contents. The scattered pieces in my mind shifted, locking into a new shape that left me both cold and certain. I gasped, then folded the paper back into the envelope.

I looked at Page and tucked it into my purse. "This changes everything."

Page tilted her head. "Meaning...what, exactly?"

I was already moving back toward the bay door and my car. The wind howled, cutting through the warehouse's warmth.

"Ellie." Page trotted after me. "You can't just drop a bomb like that and walk away!"

"I need to think." Whatever I did next, I had to keep Page as far away as possible.

"That's not an answer," Page shot back. "If it involves me, I have a right to know. Don't go all Harlan protective on me—" She stopped, swallowing the rest.

Behind us, the bay door rumbled shut.

"Right now, the less you know, the safer you are." I

pulled up the hood of my jacket, my thoughts moving three steps ahead, rearranging the whole sliding puzzle.

"And you get to decide that?" Anger reverberated through her voice.

The car unlocked with a beep.

She pulled open the passenger's side door. Stella attacked Page with her tongue as if we'd been gone for hours rather than minutes.

"For now."

FIFTEEN

Lost and Found

I spent Thursday following, observing and planning. Friday found me antsy from the moment I got up. What if I was wrong? As I drove to the bookshop, the thought gnawed at me. It would be poor Dylan all over again. I went through the evidence in my mind piece by piece and always came back with the same answer.

I would have only one shot to make my plan work. And I needed Page nowhere near the scene.

By the time darkness fell, Main Street sparkled with cheerful lights, making the Valentine's hearts from every shop window and lamppost gleam. The outside air had a sharp bite, but the inside of the shop felt almost too warm. I blamed it on the ovens that had worked overtime to get ready for tomorrow. The scent of sugar was almost cloying in the air. My skin prickled with a heat that had nothing to do with the thermostat.

"I heard Bert was back in town." I made my voice as bright and light as I could. I'd actually called Bert and found out he was on his way back home, then gently suggested that, with everything Page was going through, she might need a night out away from Brighton.

"He wants me to pick him up at the airport, then take me out to dinner in Manchester." Page's gaze flitted over the piles of decorations and romance novels and candy on the checkout counter, which left barely one square foot to checkout customers. Not that we'd had many tonight. "But there's so much to do before the Chocolate Festival tomorrow."

"Go. I'll close for you."

She clicked her tongue. "I have the displays to finish. The candy bowls to fill."

"I can do it." I took her by the shoulders, my palms damp against the angora of her neon-pink sweater, and aimed her toward the door.

She looked back at me over her shoulder and nearly poked out an eye with her heart headband. "Are you sure?"

"Better than being alone at home." I'd arranged for Evie to drop by the house to let Stella out and feed her dinner.

"True." In a flurry of movements, Page backtracked, gathering her coat, backpack and keys. She glanced at the giant bag on the floor. "There's more chocolate here, if you need it."

"I've got this." I opened the front door and urged her through, letting in a blast of cold air that had me shivering all the way down to my toes. "Go have fun. Enjoy a rare night out with Bert."

Her smile went all soft and wobbly. "Thanks, Ellie." She crossed her fingers in front of her. "Let's just hope he doesn't propose this year."

"Want me to text him?"

She waved away my offer. "It's fine. I think he finally gets that I'm not the marrying kind."

Except that Page was the marrying kind, the romantic kind, the hearts-and-flowers kind. She was just afraid of having her heart broken. The over-the-top costumes and personality were just armor because she feared that if someone saw the real her, they'd turn their back.

But if Bert had hung around with all her conditions and restrictions for thirteen years, I didn't think he'd skip out on her on their wedding day. For her sake, I hoped he kept asking.

I wanted to tell her that life was too short, that you had to take opportunities when they came your way because you might not otherwise get another chance. That marrying Bert was a way for her to expand her happiness rather than shrink it.

My hand splayed over my heart as if to hold it in. I got her fear. I got how it held her back. Because I was in the opposite boat—I was alone when I'd expected to be a duo for much longer than the thirty-some-odd years we'd had together. And that fear of being alone with no purpose left me feeling adrift.

I waited for her "batmobile" to roar down Main Street before heading to the kitchen with the bags of heart-shaped chocolates. My pulse kicked up a notch.

I placed the candy bags on the prep table and reached for the candy bowls on the shelf. *You can do this*, I told myself.

Bailey slipped in from the front.

"Looks like a quiet night." I poured chocolate hearts into a heart-shaped bowl. The candy rattled too loudly against the glass. "You can leave early, if you want."

"It's fine." She tugged at her apron strings and gave a quick shrug. "I don't really have anything going on tonight." She reached for a bowl and a bag of Kisses. "Might as well help be useful here."

"How's your mom doing?" I asked casually, heart rate jumping.

She blinked once. "My mom?"

"Your mom's Cynthia Hale, right?" I hadn't made the connection until I'd followed Bailey to the trailer park.

She gave a slow nod. "She's fine."

"Must be hard."

Her gaze narrowed. "What?"

"Watching someone you love basically squander their life. Is that why you chose to come back? To take care of her?"

"I keep an eye out for her." Her tone was a shade too careful. "I might not like what she's doing, but she's still my mother."

I got that too.

"It's cost you a lot, though, hasn't it?"

She arranged the kisses on the top layer just so. "What I've learned is that everybody's life has something crappy in it." She looked up at me, eyes hard. "Like what happened to you. Someone got drunk, and now your husband's gone."

The barb slid in, sharp and slicing. I kept my expression even, though my fingertips stuttered against the bowl's lip.

"That's true." I lined up the filled bowls to put out throughout the bookshop tomorrow morning, then riffled through the shelves.

"What are you looking for?" She balled the empty candy bags and threw them in the garbage can.

"Those chocolate-covered espresso beans. There was a half jar of them."

She stuffed her hands deep into her apron pockets. "Why?"

"I found the recipe Kady used for her cappuccino muffins, and I want to make some for the Chocolate Festival tomorrow. I figure that would make a nice tribute to her."

"Oh." Bailey shuffled jars along the shelf, the clink echoing in the room. "I think maybe Page threw them away."

If there was something Page didn't do, it was throw away perfectly good things—as anyone who visited her house could attest. *You just never know when it'll come in handy*, she'd say.

I pulled a notebook from my bag, letting Kady's recipe peek out from the top. "I think I saw some at The Farmhouse." The shop was filled with homemade goodies that I was pretty sure didn't include any chocolate-covered coffee beans. I glanced at the clock on the wall. "Just enough time to run there before it closes, if I hurry."

Bailey's hand stilled midflip through the recipe binder. "I can start those muffins for you, if you like."

"No, it's fine." I zipped my purse shut, recipe inside, pulse climbing. The kitchen seemed to shrink around me, the scent of chocolate almost overbearing. "I'll be right back."

The words tasted like walking into a dark alley without knowing what I'd find at the other end.

The trap was set. I just had to hope it didn't spring on me instead.

SIXTEEN

I See You

Harlan's voice filled my head the whole way as I racewalked to The Farmhouse. *This is dangerous, El. Let the investigators handle this.*

"They don't arrest on a hunch, and this is just a hunch."

At least let Nolan in on your plan.

"Nolan isn't you. He doesn't know me. Or trust me." And the feeling was reciprocal.

His long-suffering sigh echoed in my brain. *What's your backup?*

The small shop smelled like a country home—a mixture of goat cheese and sweet jams and savory pies. I was surprised to find a small gift bag of chocolate-covered beans, although maybe I shouldn't have, given that the Chocolate Festival started tomorrow. I bought a bag, wondering whether Bailey would still be at the bookshop when I got back, betting she would be.

What's your backup plan, Ellie? Harlan insisted on the way back, dogging my every step.

I waved his imaginary voice away as if it were a gnat.

Bailey was still in the kitchen, washing a bowl, whisk and measuring cup in slow motion. She didn't look up right away, just kept scrubbing as if the shine on the stainless steel bowl could keep her from having to see me.

"What did you make?" I asked, putting down the bag of chocolate-covered beans I'd bought on the prep table, front and center where she couldn't miss it.

"A bunch of brownie bites for sampling tomorrow. I'm hoping it'll stir the sale of the full-size brownies."

"Good idea." I sniffed the chocolate-scented air as I took off my coat, hat and scarf. "They smell really good."

"I *was* first in my class."

I took out Kady's recipe from my bag, ironing it flat against the stainless steel surface with my palm. "It's too bad you had to come back to Brighton. You could've had quite the career in the city."

"I'm making lemonade." She shrugged, circling closer on the guise of putting away the jar of cocoa. "Page gives me the freedom to experiment, so it's all good."

As she dried and put away the equipment, she watched me put together the cappuccino muffins and the espresso cream cheese spread. Her gaze felt like a camera, taking in every detail, making my head buzz with questions. What was going on in her mind?

She jabbed the whisk handle twice before she got it in the cutlery slot on the drying rack, making a discordant noise that heightened the tension in my body.

"There." With the brownie bites out of the oven, I stuffed in the muffin tin. Then I slowly put away the ingredients while Bailey's gaze tracked my every move as if she were a bloodhound. I sat on a stool, pretending to check my phone. Because Harlan was right. I should have some sort of backup plan.

I got down the bakery book and pretended to skim through, looking for another recipe to make, double-checking my theory.

After the muffins had finished baking, I broke one in half, steam rising from the cakey texture, the scent of chocolate, cream and coffee filling the air. I spread it with the espresso cream cheese, which oozed right into the warm muffin. "Sit," I said. "You've been on your feet all day."

She sat tentatively on the other stool. I handed her a muffin half like an offering, not a weapon. "What do you think?"

She took a bite, chewing slowly. "They're okay."

But her gaze remained fixed on the muffin, refusing to meet mine.

"Just okay?" I took a bite, not really tasting anything. "What would you have done differently?"

She frowned down at the muffin as if it were a piece of evidence at a crime scene. "I'd have backed off on the sugar and added a touch of cinnamon."

Which was exactly what I'd changed—adding an extra quarter cup of sugar and leaving out the cinnamon. "Because you made this recipe first."

"Nah, not my recipe." She crumpled the cupcake liner and pitched it into the garbage. "Can't remember where I've had something similar."

"It hurts when you put in all the work and someone takes all the credit."

She reached for the bowl I'd used and took it to the sink. "I have no idea what you're talking about."

"You're not the only one, you know."

She squirted some dish soap into the bowl. "The only one what?"

"Who's had a recipe copycatted by Kady."

She sprayed water into the bowl, soap fomenting into a ball of bubbles. "Even back in high school, Kady was an entitled princess who never had to work for anything."

"While you've had to scrape and scrimp all of your life. I bet you went to baking school on a scholarship."

She snorted and reached for a scrubber. "Wow, you should be a detective or something with those deductive skills."

"What I couldn't figure out is when Kady could've taken your recipe. You went to baking school in New York, not Hopewell. You worked for a catering company and did some temp work. None of those jobs gave you a chance to make your own recipes. And how did you find out she'd copied your recipe?"

She whirled around and faced me, skin pinkening fast. Her voice vibrated low and sharp. "You don't know anything."

"I'd like to." I tilted my head. "I know you've had some hard luck—"

"Save it." She turned back to the sink and scrubbed. "I know you're trying to find someone other than Page to take the fall for Kady's death. Just because I come from the wrong side of the tracks doesn't mean you can pin it on me."

"Unless you did it."

"Like you said, why would I do it?" She jammed the bowl onto the drying rack. "I haven't seen the girl since high school."

"But you did. The day you came for the interview. She came in as you left. Page kept a record."

"So?"

Once again, I took the photocopy of the cappuccino muffin recipe I'd made out of my purse. The original was safely stowed at home where Nolan would find it if something happened to me. I slid it across the prep table so that Bailey could see the reverse-engineering work that had happened. "Eerie, isn't it, how accurate she was?"

Bailey's fingers twitched before she even touched the page—as if her body recognized it before her mind could form an excuse. Then she brushed it aside with the back of her hand as if the recipe were nothing but crumbs. "Lucky guess for a lucky girl."

"Why did you set up Page to take the fall?"

She reached for a sponge and scrubbed the counter. "I have no idea what you're talking about."

"The way you displayed Kady with the rolling pin you used to knock her out, Page's glasses, keys and note…"

Bailey kept cleaning the counter as if her life depended on it.

"Kady didn't die from the blow to the back of the head," I continued. "I'm guessing that was just the heat of the moment. Then when you saw her lying there. Maybe you even realized that she couldn't wake up, or you'd be in trouble. So you strangled her."

She wrung out the sponge in the sink and placed it back in the caddy. "Well, it looks like we're all done for the night. I'll leave you to lock up."

"Sleeping in your car must get awfully cold in winter."

She just smiled, a smile that had zero warmth and too much bitterness. "What? You've been spying on me now?"

"I know what it's like to lose your dream, to expect life to turn out one way, then have the rug pulled out from under you."

She slipped on her drab-olive coat like armor. *Invisible*, I thought.

And that's when I knew exactly why she'd set up Page.

She hiked her battered bag to her shoulder. "I'm exactly where I want to be."

I lifted my hands, taking in the whole store. "But if Page goes to prison, you lose it all."

"The bookstore will go on. Someone will buy it. Or you'll run it for her until she gets out. You two are thick like that."

"Doesn't guarantee they'll keep you on as baker."

She gave half a shrug. "I always land on my feet."

"Even a cat has only nine lives. I think you're on your last one."

"You can't prove anything."

"The one thing I'm good at is seeing patterns." I pulled another sheet from my purse. "I went through the applications and saw yours."

For the first time a flicker of fear flashed across her face, there and gone. "So?"

"Did you know Page had picked you for the job but felt obliged to hire Kady?"

Her breath went short and shallow. "That's the way it goes. Some people get all the breaks, whether they deserve them or not."

"When you bake, you hum. It's a happy sound that comes from deep inside. You care about your work. It's not just a job."

Her gaze darted to the muffins, then back to me. Her eyes shone with tears.

"I see you, Bailey." In the end, that's all anyone wanted —to be seen, to be loved, to feel as if they mattered. And Bailey had felt none of those growing up with a mother who cared only for herself.

"You work so hard, you feel it in your bones. And then someone just waltzes in and gets the chance you thought was yours. It's not fair. That kind of hurt leaves a hole you can't ever bake over."

I was learning that the hard way. No number of muffins or cookies or pies was going to take away the pain of losing Harlan.

Her jaw shifted as if she were chewing on words she couldn't swallow.

I reached out and placed one of my hands over hers. "It must have hurt when you came in last Saturday and Page didn't recognize you."

She swallowed hard. "She probably did a lot of inter-views. And it was ages ago. Why would she have remem-bered me?"

"Because you were the only one who brought in a sample." I nudged a cappuccino muffin toward her on the table. "A batch of these."

SEVENTEEN

Justice Served

"Page was so impressed," I said, nudging the cappuccino muffin closer, "that she made a note on your application."

Bailey stared at the muffin on the prep table. Not moving. Not blinking. The same look she'd given the recipe earlier—as if it were dangerous to touch. The slow *tick-tock* of the clock beat out of time to the fast hammer of my heart.

"I know you didn't mean to hurt Kady," I said, hoping my fingers hit the right keys on my phone. "But she just wouldn't listen. And it all happened so fast. They'll take that into consideration."

Bailey's grip tightened around the strap of her battered bag. "She just wouldn't admit she'd stolen my recipe."

Gooseflesh pebbled my skin as I took a small step

toward her. The soles of my boots hissed along the tile floor like a warning. The sweet scent of cocoa offered a sharp contrast to the sour dread that filled me. I softened my voice. "You've had to carry this burden for days. All alone."

Bailey's laugh was short and brittle. She glanced at the cooling racks filled with brownie bites, cookies and muffins. Then at the knives in the block on the counter, their shiny handles catching the harsh kitchen light. Her fingers twitched as if she were drawn to the weapon, but she didn't reach.

The fingers of both hands dove into her perfectly neat bun, pulling it apart. "It wasn't supposed to happen that way." Her voice cracked, fragile like thin ice. "I just wanted my recipe back. It's the *one* thing that was mine."

She caved against the counter as if she needed the support. "I tried talking to her. Twice." Bailey sneered. "And she dismissed me like I was nothing."

"When that didn't work, you tried setting her up as having stolen Marissa's recipe." I opened the bake book to one of the lighter-print pages. "These are your recipes. The ones you added to the book. When did you put Marissa's in here?"

"I figured Marissa would set her straight since she'd already had to deal with one theft." Her lips curled into a small smile. "I made some cupcakes and brought one over to Marissa, knowing she'd get Mad Hatter angry."

"But that didn't work. You saw your muffins for sale again." I took a step closer. "So you came after closing, when you knew Kady would be alone."

"She'd have to listen then. She'd get that what she was doing was hurting others."

"Others who didn't have all the advantages she had." I took another step closer. "Then what happened?"

"She told me she had bigger worries than a stupid recipe." She gritted her teeth. "And she turned her back on me."

"That's when you hit her with the rolling pin."

Bailey shook her head in slow arcs. "I just wanted her to look at me."

"To see you. To see how she'd hurt you."

Tears poured down Bailey's face. "She wasn't moving." She swiped at the tears with the back of her hand, but they kept flowing. "And I got scared."

"Then you got mad all over again because if Page had hired you in the first place, none of this would've happened."

"She betrayed me. They both did." Bailey was crying so hard her whole body spasmed with the grief.

"You threw her in the dumpster and then stuffed those chocolate-covered coffee beans in her mouth."

"She had them out. She was making *my* recipe for the festival! That crowning touch? That was *my* idea."

"What about the garbage bag? Why didn't you just use one of Page's?"

"It broke, so I had to use one from my car."

"Where you store your possessions because you can't live at home." I'd peered into her car, seen the sleeping bag on the back seat, seen the collection of garbage bags filled with her meager possessions, the passenger's side window taped over with clear plastic sheeting. I'd driven by the single-wide listed as her address, seen the neglect. I couldn't imagine any child growing up there.

"Not with all the dirtbags my mom brings home."

"I'm so sorry, Bailey. Life's really been unfair to you." I felt for her, for the injustice, for the favoritism that had colored her world. I reached for her and pulled her into a hug. She resisted for a moment, then collapsed and cried on my shoulder.

"I'd just lost everything," Bailey said through her tears. "Someone broke into my car, took the few things I had that had any value." Her voice stuttered. "They stole my grandmother's antique recipe box with all the recipes she passed on to me. They'd mean nothing to anyone else. To me, they were everything. And then Kady..." Bailey gulped in air as if she were starving. "She had everything. Why couldn't she give me back what was mine? Wouldn't even admit she'd done anything wrong. I —I just lost it."

"Understandable." A person could take only so much before cracking, but killing Kady had taken it one step too far. "Tell you what, I'll go with you to the police, and I'll explain—"

Bailey pushed back from me so hard that I stumbled backward a step. "No! I'm not going to the police!"

She grabbed a knife from the block, held it tight by the hilt by her shoulder, ready to plunge it into my heart. I could taste the blood. I could feel the brush of death. Since Harlan had died, part of me had wanted to join him, just to end the constant pain that gripped my heart. But at this moment, one thing became clear: I wanted to live.

I reached an arm forward, palm up. "You're going to give me the knife."

Her whole face scrunched. "Now you've gone and made things worse."

I caught movement by the kitchen door. Nolan stood just out of the pale light, shadowed but poised like a coiled spring ready to leap. His hand hovered near his belt. A rush of relief went through me. He'd deciphered my message.

I gave him what I hoped was an almost imperceptible shake of my head. *Not yet*, I willed him to understand. *She doesn't want to hurt me. She's just scared.*

I softened my voice, letting it drop low and flow like a balm. "You're scared of what might happen."

"You think me walking into the police station is going to fix anything?" Her eyes glittered with rage. "They'll see me as a monster. Nothing else. The lowlife who killed the princess."

"I'll make them see your pain." I took a breath, feeling her despair. "Keeping that pain buried inside...that's a prison too."

The hand holding the knife trembled. "I just wanted my recipe back."

I nodded. "You wanted justice for yourself."

"And she wouldn't give it to me," Bailey whispered, tears rolling freely down her cheeks.

A soft creak sounded from the door as if the old building were settling in the cold night. My heart thudded so hard I was surprised no one else could hear it. My gaze went to Nolan, who stood steady in the shadows, waiting. *Not yet.*

I stepped a little closer and dropped my voice even lower. "You don't have to be afraid anymore, Bailey. You're not alone. I'm here for you."

Bailey rocked on her heels, torn, the fight draining from her face in ragged waves. Her gaze took in the knife in her hand, and she looked at it as if she had no idea how it'd gotten there. The room went impossibly still, except for the faint scrape of her trembling fingernails on the counter.

"I'll lose everything," she said. "My freedom. My work. The little bit of pride I have left."

I reached out, hand hovering close to Bailey's elbow, offering her a lifeline. "I'll be there. Every step. You're not alone."

Bailey's breath hitched, her gaze piercing mine, finding truth. Then, finally, as if the last thread holding her together had snapped, she leaned into my arms. "I didn't mean for any of this to happen. I just wanted my recipe back."

"I've got you," I said, and gathered her into my arms.

"I'm tired, so tired." The knife clattered to the floor, and she held on to me for dear life with both arms.

Keeping his voice calm and gentle, Nolan stepped behind Bailey and said, "Bailey Hale, you're under arrest for the murder of Kady Chilton."

IN THE SMALL INTERVIEW ROOM, THE HARSH fluorescent lights buzzed overhead, casting long shadows across the table where I sat, hands folded in my lap. They'd finished the interview with Bailey. She'd insisted I stay with

HER, AND I'D MADE HER A PROMISE, SO NOLAN had bent the rules.

She confessed to killing Kady in the heat of anger. She also confessed to drugging Erik, compounding one mistake with another. Everyone had noticed his growing sadness, so she'd thought his suicide would've close dthe case. Except that the dose hadn't been strong enough to kill him.

She would stay the night in Brighton PD's one holding cell and be transported to Valley Street in Manchester in the morning. After she'd left the room, Nolan had taken my statement. And now he paced behind me, giving me the third degree.

"I'm serious, Ellie." Nolan stopped and faced me. His voice was low and sharp. "You could've gotten killed tonight. You should've called me when you first thought Bailey might have killed Kady."

"If you'd been more forthcoming with information, maybe it wouldn't have come to this."

A growl came from low in his chest. "I was trying to protect you and Page! I never thought Page killed Kady, but I had to make sure I followed every piece of evidence, especially *because* Page was involved."

"And how would you have responded if I'd told you about my hunch? You'd have said you can't convict on a gut feeling." Just as Harlan would have. But still. I may have judged Nolan a tad too harshly. He was trying to help. "I needed to be sure." My clasped hands slid toward him on the tabletop. "So you would take me seriously."

Both arms shot out to his sides. "She held a knife at you!"

I shrugged a shoulder. "She didn't want to use it. She was just scared."

"You were lucky."

"I called you as soon as I knew for sure."

He shook his head. "That phone bit? You call that a proper warning?"

"I call that using what I had at hand." I sighed. "Bailey's just a lost soul drowning in fear, regret and so much loss. She didn't mean to kill Kady."

He opened his mouth, and I held up a hand. "I know it doesn't excuse what she did, but that recipe box that was stolen, that recipe she concocted, they were her link to the only warmth she's ever felt in her life. When her grandmother died, all that disappeared. And that recipe was her pride and joy. The one thing that was hers. Taking that box, that recipe, that was as grievous in her state of mind as murder."

Nolan pulled up a chair and sat, rubbing his temples. "If anything had happened to you..." He blew out a breath. "Losing Harlan—"

My heart went heavy. "I know. I've felt lost since it happened."

The room grew thick with our shared grief.

"But watching Bailey fall apart—" I shook my head. "I haven't cared whether I lived or not since Harlan died. Only the kids have kept me going. But when I had that knife pointed at my heart, the one thing I knew for sure was that I wasn't ready to die yet."

Nolan's eerie golden gaze studied mine. "I'm glad."

Healing wasn't about forgetting or moving on in big leaps. Maybe it was about taking small steps, one at a time, even when the path was unclear.

I gave him a watery smile. "One step at a time."

EIGHTEEN

A New Day

Saturday dawned with glorious sunshine, filling the world with bright winter cheer. With the Chocolate Festival officially opening this morning, the bookshop and café would hum with activity. Over-sugared, over-caffeinated, over-bright people would buzz around Main Street, seeking their next fix of chocolate. All leading to the Sweetheart Dance at the community center tonight.

Stella at my side, a bouquet of pink Gerbera daisies in my hand, I strolled through the shoveled pathways at the cemetery and stopped at Harlan's grave marker in the shade of an oak tree. Kneeling, I swept away the cover of snow. Then I placed the flowers on the stone. Stella nosed around, sniffing at the snow, unaware of her favorite person's final resting place.

"I know you think flowers are silly but they're an offering from the heart. I love you, Harlan. I will always love you. I miss you every single day. And I need to find a way to have purpose without you. Not just for the kids. But for me too."

A cardinal landed on a branch of the nearby oak, singing, and it sounded strangely like "When You Kiss Me." I chuckled, knuckling away tears from both cheeks at the memory of Harlan singing to me. I put my fingertips to my lips, missing him reeling me in, missing his kiss. "He's as off-key as you were."

Petting Stella sitting beside me, I let the bird finish his song, said goodbye and retraced my steps to the car.

As soon as I walked into the bookshop, Page grabbed me. The place looked magical with its twinkling heart-shaped fairy lights, curated displays of love-themed books and paper hearts hanging from the ceiling. "You won't believe this, but Bailey didn't show this morning!" She stabbed a finger at her phone, as if that would make her appear. "And she's not answering her phone."

"About that," I said. Stella hopped around Page, seeking attention. "I think you're going to have to look for another baker."

"Why?" Page grumbled and rubbed the spot by Stella's tail that had the dog groaning with delight. I told her what had happened last night at the café.

"Wow," Page said, shaking her head. "All this time, we were feeding her information and she was using it to tighten the evidence against me."

She grabbed both my arms. "If you hadn't believed in me, she'd have gotten her way. I'd have been charged with Kady's murder."

"I wasn't going to let that happen."

"I owe you," she said, gaze serious. "Big time. But I am not looking forward to interviewing bakers again. I've struck out twice now."

"Maybe third time's the charm," I said, leading her to the checkout counter. Stella plopped into her bed. "Tell you what."

Page's eyebrows rose.

"I'll come work for you part time until you can find someone to run the café."

"You will?" Page squeezed me into a hug so hard I could hardly breathe. "Thank you, thank you, thank you."

I didn't know what would come next, only that I was ready to move forward, one step at a time. And that moving forward didn't mean I loved Harlan any less.

The alarm on Page's watch went off. Her face brightened and she smoothed the material of her garish heart-covered skirt. She crowed at the line that was already forming at the door. "Time to open!"

———

Thank you for reading! While the story is fresh in your mind, I'd be eternally grateful if you took a few minutes to write a review. Your review helps more than you think.

All the best,
Sylvie

Bailey's Cappuccino Muffins

WITH ESPRESSO CREAM CHEESE SPREAD

Prep Time: 15 minutes

Cook Time: 20 minutes

Servings: 12 muffins

Muffin Ingredients:

- 2 cups flour
- 3/4 cup sugar
- 2 1/2 teaspoons baking powder
- 1/2 teaspoon ground cinnamon
- 1/2 teaspoon salt
- 1 cup milk, room temperature
- 2 tablespoons instant coffee powder, unbrewed
- 1/2 cup butter, melted
- 1 egg, room temperature

- 1 teaspoon vanilla
- 3/4 cup mini semisweet chocolate chips

Spread Ingredients

- 8 oz cream cheese, room temperature
- 2 tablespoons sugar
- 1 teaspoon instant espresso powder, unbrewed
- 1 teaspoon vanilla
- 1/2 cup mini semisweet chocolate chips

Instructions

For the Muffins:

1. Preheat the oven to 375°F.
2. Combine the flour, sugar, baking powder, cinnamon and salt in a large bowl.
3. In another bowl, whisk the milk and instant coffee until the powder is dissolved.
4. Add the melted butter, egg, and vanilla to the milk/coffee mixture.
5. Stir the wet ingredients into the flour mixture.
6. Fold in the chocolate chips.
7. Line a muffin pan with paper liners and fill each cup 3/4 of the way.

8. Bake for 18-20 minutes, or until a toothpick comes out with crumbs.

For the Cream Cheese Spread

1. In a food processor, blend all the spread ingredients.
2. Chill the spread in the fridge until you're ready to serve.
3. Spread it onto warm muffins.
4. Enjoy!

Vip Reader

Want to keep up with what's going on in Brighton Village? Join my VIP Readers List today. The newsletter comes out (more or less) once a month and contains book updates, behind-the-scenes tidbits, recipes, specials and extras only my VIP readers receive. Go to https://sylviekurtz.com/mailing-list and sign up now!

Book Clubs

LET'S MEET!

Is your book club planning to read one of my books? I love to talk with readers. If you would like me to visit your book club, a 30-minute online or phone visit with your club is always free.

Just use my contact form to let me know about your gathering, or if you have any questions about how it works.

Can't wait to chat!

Remembering Red Thunder

Red Thunder Reckoning

Into the Fire

Detour

The Seekers Series

Heart of a Hunter

Mask of a Hunter

Eye of a Hunter

Pride of a Hunter

Spirit of a Hunter

Honor of a Hunter

Action-Adventure Romance

Ms. Longshot

Paranormal Romance

Broken Wings

Silver Shadows

Holiday Romance

A Little Christmas Magic

Sylvie writes stories that celebrate family, friends and food. She believes organic dark chocolate is an essential nutrient, likes to knit with soft yarn, and justifies watching movies that require a box of tissues by knitting baby blankets. She has written 28 novels in various genres.

Her first Harlequin Intrigue, *One Texas Night*, was a 1999 *Romantic Times* nominee for Best First Category Romance and a finalist for a Booksellers Best Award. Her Silhouette Special Edition, *A Little Christmas Magic,* was a 2001 Readers' Choice Award Finalist and a Waldenbooks bestseller. *Remembering Red Thunder* was a 2002 Romantic Times Nominee for Best Intrigue. *Broken Wings* was an RWA Golden Heart finalist. She was a 2005, 2007 and 2008 *Romantic Times* nominee for Lifetime Achievement for Series Romantic Adventure. Twin Star Entertainment optioned *Ms. Longshot* as a possible TV movie.

For more details, visit https://sylviekurtz.com.

A small press bound by the belief that every voice matters.

Sign up for our newsletter to learn about new releases and more.
https://oliver-heberbooks.com/subscribe/

Follow us on social media:

facebook.com/oliverheberbooks

instagram.com/oliverheberbooks

amazon.com/oliverheberbooks

youtube.com/@OliverHeberBooksPublisher